Trace kept a firm hold on her.

The sheer wonder at having her in his arms again was juxtaposed by the thick protective material between them and the reality that they were standing in the woods mere yards from where a sniper had hidden less than an hour before.

Even as an awareness in the back of his mind recognized they were still in danger, something more present—and far more fierce—beat in his blood.

He needed this. Desperately.

Because one wrong move and she'd have died today.

He knew he should pay attention to all of that.

But all he wanted was Nic.

And these quiet, nearly desperate moments to hold her close and make them both remember what had burned so bright and clear between them.

How he felt when he was with her.

Free in a way he'd never experienced before or since.

Trace pushed every one of those emotions into the kiss. It was hot and carnal and oddly sweet at the same time.

Because whatever he'd remembered of her, nothing could compare to having her in his arms once more.

Danger be damned.

Dear Reader,

Welcome to the start of my new series, Wyoming Warriors. Trace Withrow is a man without a mission. Ex-CIA, he gave up his DC life in favor of a small, barely there dot on the map—Liar's Gulch, Wyoming—to raise, train and rescue horses on a four-hundred-acre ranch. While his focus is on the animals, Trace and his ex-SEAL brother, Garner, and their associate, former Vegas PD detective Jake, still selectively take on cases. It's work that matters.

Nicola Miles has always been a model CIA operative. Trace's "toss the rule book out the window" approach never quite worked for her, but it was their partnership that led to a steamy affair and nearly incinerated them both. Trace is the last person she'd go to for a favor, but she knows he's the only one who can help her find a missing child. Especially since she believes the child is in danger because of a fellow agent running a bad op.

With his life and his heart on the line, Trace has an overwhelming need to keep Nic safe. He lost her once and still hasn't recovered. Could he survive if he lost her again?

I hope you enjoy this high-stakes jaunt to Wyoming. And I hope you agree that Trace and Nic deserve one more shot at their happily-ever-after.

Best,

Addison Fox

RENEGADE REUNION

ADDISON FOX

ROMANTIC SUSPENSE

Harlequin®
ROMANTIC SUSPENSE™

Recycling programs for this product may not exist in your area.

ISBN-13: 978-1-335-50274-2

Renegade Reunion

Copyright © 2025 by Frances Karkosak

Harlequin Enterprises ULC
22 Adelaide St. West, 41st Floor
Toronto, Ontario M5H 4E3, Canada
www.Harlequin.com

Printed in Lithuania

MIX
Paper | Supporting responsible forestry
FSC® C021394

Addison Fox is a lifelong romance reader, addicted to happily-ever-afters. After discovering she found as much joy writing about romance as she did reading it, she's never looked back. Addison lives in New York with an apartment full of books, a laptop that's rarely out of sight and a wily beagle who keeps her running. You can find her at her home on the web at addisonfox.com or on Facebook (Facebook.com/addisonfoxauthor) and X (@addisonfox).

Books by Addison Fox

Harlequin Romantic Suspense

Wyoming Warriors

Renegade Reunion

New York Harbor Patrol

Danger in the Depths
Peril in the Shallows
Threats in the Deep

The Coltons of Owl Creek

Guarding Colton's Secrets

The Coltons of New York

Under Colton's Watch

Midnight Pass, Texas

The Cowboy's Deadly Mission
Special Ops Cowboy
Under the Rancher's Protection
Undercover K-9 Cowboy
Her Texas Lawman

Visit the Author Profile page at Harlequin.com.

For Beth and Eric.

A life in service protecting others is an incredible sacrifice, both for the one who protects and the one who waits each day for their return. Your love, support and belief in each other is an inspiration.

Chapter 1

"And just as it always does, water seeks the lowest level. Just like you, you hungover idiot."

Trace Withrow knelt down beside the rushing stream, fresh with spring rain and winter snowmelt, and washed his face. The water was freezing, which meant it did wonders for the hangover he was still sporting. Even if it froze his fingers in the process.

Damn, but his friends knew how to throw a party. And welcoming home one of their own had certainly been worth every minute of his monumentally painful ride this morning. It couldn't, however, erase one unalienable fact.

"I'm getting too old for this crap."

Trace sat up, wiping the ice-cold water from his face. His horse, Magnum, was seemingly oblivious to his pain as he bent his head, drinking from the same stream. Although Magnum was a faithful companion and Trace trusted him implicitly, the horse had little in the way of equine compassion.

A trait Trace admired in spades.

Magnum lifted his head, his dark brown gaze hard and unyielding. Although the Arabian had never gone all Mr. Ed on him, that look spoke more than a thousand words.

Get your sorry butt in gear and let's finish up our work.

"So noted."

Trace got to his feet, the vast, sprawling Wyoming mountains spreading out in all directions. It was a far cry from DC—what wasn't, outside the Beltway?—and that had only added to its appeal.

Liar's Gulch, Wyoming. A vast, Western wilderness that had surprisingly become home. And, despite its name, had far more good people than the liars, backstabbers and power players he'd called colleagues back in Washington.

Liar's Gulch had also become his haven. His respite from a life that he still sharply remembered, even if the edges had gone blessedly dull as he healed out in the big, wide-open West, running a horse-training-and-rescue operation on the four hundred acres that he now called home.

The air around them was quiet as Trace gave one last stretch before moving back to Magnum. He'd nearly placed a foot in the stirrups, ready to mount, when something stopped him.

A stillness, maybe?

It made little sense, but he'd trained too long and too hard to ignore the hairs that stood up on the back of his neck. And he'd managed to stay alive because he—never once—doubted them.

Patting Magnum's neck in a casual gesture, Trace considered the gun at his waistband and the other clutch piece at his ankle. He could have both in hand and firing in less than two seconds.

Which was two seconds too long if whatever had him in its crosshairs decided to move.

And that left him with only one choice.

Swinging around as he drew his gun, Trace faced off against his enemy.

And laid eyes on the only woman he'd ever loved.

* * *

Nicola Miles held her position, the safety off her gun and her stance fixed as she stared down Trace Withrow. Realistically, she didn't want to shoot him. His body was way too fine to put a bullet into if she could help it.

But sometimes fate had other ideas.

"Nic." The edges of his lips twitched, but other than that slight movement, the rest of him was eerily still.

"Jackass." She meant it in greeting and had to hold back the wince when she registered the extra-sharp note in her voice. She knew her upper hand was tenuous at best, and giving even the slightest sense that she was at a disadvantage simply would not do.

To his credit, he didn't seem to register the greeting, but neither did he relax his own stance or lower the piece in his hands that matched her own.

Old habits died hard.

"This is a surprise."

"I don't doubt that."

And she didn't. When they'd left each other two years ago, there had been a finality to the parting that hadn't characterized their other battles. Fights that had always ended in the sweetest sort of détente.

But not that one.

That one had been nuclear in its destruction. The sort where even the cockroaches died and mass-produced cheese actually melted.

The one that ended it all.

"To what do I owe the pleasure?" Those compelling gray eyes of his were as inscrutable as ever. So was his tone. Flat. Uncompromising.

Just like the man.

Traits she admired in a colleague and an opponent that were wildly out of place in a lover and a life partner.

Unless you added *uncompromising in his thoroughness* when he loved her.

Nicola shook off the heated images that brought. She would not think of the hot, thick air that had filled their humid hotel room in a run-down section of Buenos Aires. Nor would she think about the impossible cold they'd fought off in the wilds of Siberia, with a small fire, two thick coats and only each other to stay warm.

She knew this man.

Knew his body and his mind, his values and his blind spots.

And he knew her. Knew her in ways no one else ever had or, she now keenly understood, ever would.

"You going to make me ask again?" One lone eyebrow rose above those eyes she knew so well. So well, in fact, that she still dreamed about them.

Regularly.

"I need your help."

"By holding me at gunpoint?"

Nicola allowed her gaze to flash ever so briefly to the cold metal at the end of her hands. "It's an effective enticement."

"So is sex, but I don't see you offering that."

Damn him, he knew just what to say to get under her skin. "I'd rather put a bullet in your ass than touch it."

He took a few steps closer, his voice like silk, even as his own gun stayed firmly in place. "You didn't always feel that way. Even at your maddest, you never felt that way."

"Things change."

"Actually, most things don't change." Without warning, Trace dropped his gun. "Not one single bit."

She'd never been afraid of handling a gun. A fact that wasn't only handy but absolutely necessary in her line of work. But she'd never been comfortable holding one steady on someone who posed no threat.

And while she might understand how threatening, tough and all around badass Trace Withrow could be when riled, this moment wasn't it.

Her own gun fell to her side before she took another precious moment to put on the safety. A moment that gave him the advantage—if he wanted it—to grab his clutch piece.

A moment—if he took it—that would give her some perverse pleasure in battling him hand to hand.

Yet in the end, it was a moment that passed without any further movement, threatening or otherwise.

"Why are you here, Nic?"

"I told you. I need your help."

"How'd you find me?"

The question was flat, devoid of emotion, which was almost enough to push her own ire back to the surface. She didn't want to need him, damn it. Didn't want his help.

Even if she had no say in the matter.

Add on the fact that she was still smarting from those sexy, overwhelming flashbacks, and she would have done anything else on earth but stand before him, vulnerable and alone. She could still picture his naked body, a towel around his lean, whipcord hips, his inky-black hair still dark from a shower, just like it was now at the edges. She'd watched him dip his head in that rushing stream, shivering to herself when she imagined him bracing against the cold of the water.

Thoughts of the water had led right into images of him fresh out of a shower, which had then blended with memories of the cold, and then her mind was right back in Siberia and…

Oh, it had been a long twenty-four months.

"Well? I deserve to know."

His question still hanging between them, she considered her approach. It would be so easy to poke at his pride, dismissing the question and, with a laugh, suggest just how quickly she'd found his location.

Only it would be a lie.

When Trace Withrow had walked out of the CIA, he'd meant it. No matter how well she knew how to use the tools at her disposal, the man had been nearly impossible to find. In the end, it had been the fact that she knew him—and remembered a throwaway conversation on assignment in Geneva. He'd talked of a small corner of Wyoming where he loved to fish while on his personal holidays away from DC.

His dark, husky voice had been filled with awe as he spoke of nature's bounty. She'd only ever heard that tone when they made love. When his lips were pressed against the shell of her ear, his large body finding a rhythm over hers. In those precious hours together, his voice had held both the promise of pleasure and the wonder at what flared and flamed between them.

She'd taken it for granted at the time. Had believed the pleasure was something born of the moment. A product of their intense jobs and schedules, the work they did grueling and satisfying all at the same time.

They'd been attracted to one another from the start, and she'd entered into the affair well aware neither of them were relationship material. She'd always known that about herself, cementing the truth of it once she entered the rarefied air of the Central Intelligence Agency.

The CIA had offered all she ever wanted. Since the day she'd gotten the agency as her group study project in high school civics, she'd recognized it as the perfect place for her. A place where she could do work that mattered. Where she would matter.

It was an idea that had enticed, even as it was in short supply in her young life. After being bumped from place to place as a child, she'd nearly run away out of the foster system.

Until the Bakers.

They showed up around the same time as that civics class.

Nic wasn't a big believer in fate, but figured someone, somewhere was looking out for her when, at fourteen, she'd finally found a permanent home with a sweet older couple. They'd given her a soft place to land, with minimal judgment and even fewer rules, but a roof, three squares and a gentle insistence she get an education.

Through that education, she'd found her true calling.

Once that civics project had finished, she'd researched the hell out of the CIA on her own. Where most of her fellow students were hunting up the latest makeup tutorial or endless photo-filled articles on their favorite boy band, Nic scoured the internet for details on the CIA. She'd trained body and mind, working up to five miles a day for her daily run and acing all her classes to get into a good college in DC.

It never once dawned on her to deviate from her path. Nor had she ever questioned that she was made for dangerous assignments with the highest of stakes. Those stakes never bothered her because they provided the very best outcomes should they succeed.

Until Trace.

He'd been as driven as she, yet he knew how to play. How to walk away when the situation got so intense it singed you from every angle. And how to give perspective to the work so that even when it was all-consuming, it wasn't everything.

"I'm not asking again, Nic. How'd you find me?"

The smooth, casual attitude had vanished, leaving behind the reality of who and what he was. Trace Withrow might wear any number of facades, but he was an inherently dangerous man, with or without a loaded gun in his hand.

"You talked about this place. That endless week we spent in Geneva staking out those insurgents. It was a mindless, empty conversation about four coffees into our day."

His eyes narrowed. "The one about vacation spots. You were particularly keen on Maui, as I recall."

"Have you ever met anyone, ever, who doesn't love Maui?"

He ignored her stall tactic. "And that's how you found me here?"

Damn it, she couldn't tell him the truth. How that conversation had haunted her long after they'd caught the insurgents. That there was something wistful in his voice when he spoke of the mountains and the land and the endlessly clear streams. Something that had drawn her in and made her think that there was a place in the world where she wasn't a reject foster kid. Where nature was bright enough and pure enough to wash away any number of sins.

And where, if she was with him, she might actually be worthy of him.

* * *

He remembered that conversation. That stakeout. That time in his life. He remembered it all with a clarity that was so vivid it hurt to breathe through the memories.

What he couldn't reconcile was that she had remembered.

Trace had never doubted Nicola Miles in any way. Her intelligence. Her courage. Or her willingness to do what was needed to achieve their goals.

But it was humbling—even as stubborn hope sparked in his chest and through the raging headache that pounded his temples—to realize he might have underestimated his impact on her.

Had she not shared the memory from that stakeout, he'd have continued on in his beliefs. The ones that had haunted him for two years now. The ones that said he was the hopeless fool.

He'd been the one to fall in love. To break the unspoken agreement between them that they'd use the sheer combustion that fueled their encounters as a pleasurable way to blow off steam while on assignment. Nothing more.

Only now, he had to wonder.

Had she felt something?

Or was she just that damn good? Remembering a throwaway comment in a throwaway conversation on an endless stakeout.

Disgusted with himself for opening the "deeper meaning" door even a crack, Trace moved a few steps forward. Nic's vivid blue—almost crystal—gaze never left his, nor did she move back a step.

This was a woman who knew how to stand her ground.

A fact that delighted him and infuriated him in equal measure.

He gave himself another few beats to look his fill—that vivid blue, the sweep of blond that arced behind her ear, the firm line of her jaw that was so sharp it should have been a warning—before offering the denial she had to have anticipated. "We don't have the same boss anymore. And since there's only about three planks still holding up the bridge I tried to burn, no one back at Uncle Sam's ranch is going to give you a parade for coming to find me."

"No one knows I'm here."

"If you actually believe that, then let me sell you those three remaining planks, sweetheart."

"No, Trace. No one knows."

He'd had a long time to come to grips with what he knew about her, but one thing he'd never doubted was her honesty. She had an unwavering faith in her colleagues and the organization she'd devoted her life to for over a decade. It had been a point of contention between them— one they'd never come close to reconciling—and it had only added to their implosion at the end.

"Since when does Nicola Miles work outside the auspices of the mighty CIA?"

Her gaze darted down toward the rocky scrub grass beneath their feet before determinedly shooting back up to rest on his face. "I'm not working outside anything."

"You are if you're telling me the truth. The CIA takes care of its own. It doesn't need help from ex-agents who left on bad terms."

"This has nothing to do with the CIA. This has to do with me."

"You are the CIA, Nic. You have been since the day you walked in the door. Nothing could dislodge that boulder of trust and self-righteousness off your shoulder."

For a long time, he'd accepted it. Oh, he'd poked at her

plenty about it, but he'd trusted that she was smart enough and well trained enough to hold her own, no matter the situation. And if she had a deep-seated belief that the organization she worked for was focused on fundamentally doing good, what did it hurt?

It was better than his piss-poor attitude. The one that had burned those bridge planks, one by one, in his fifteen years with the agency. Because while she liked to believe her fellow agents were fundamentally good, made even better by the structure and intelligence and security around them, Trace opted for the opposing view.

Anyone who chose the life—who understood the shadowy underbelly of how the world worked—wasn't immune from those shadows themselves.

She still stood close enough to touch. Close enough he could feel the heat emanating off her body in the cold morning air. Close enough he could see the throb of her pulse against the delicate skin of her throat.

But it was the whisper, thick and nearly strangled in that morning air, that caught him up as cleanly as the fish he loved to drag from the river. "I think you might be right, Trace. Have always been right."

"About what?"

"There are traitors in our midst. Whether by choice or by consequence, I don't know. But I do know I can't fight them alone." She hesitated, before adding, "I can't fight an enemy I can't see."

"And you think I can?"

"I think you always have. I just never wanted to believe you."

"What changed your mind?"

"It's a kid this time. She's fifteen and brilliant and—"

She broke off, but there was something in the hesitation that told Trace all he needed to know.

Somehow, some way, her case had turned personal.

And that was the biggest danger an agent could face. He'd learned that lesson the hard way, and now it appeared she had, too.

"Why this kid?"

"She's a computer genius, and she was my asset. I was protecting her, and she vanished three days ago."

"Runaway?"

"It was made to look like it. I don't believe it."

"Why not? Genius kids have a lot of attitude. And at fifteen, you think you can do anything. Who wants to be cooped up in a crappy safe house, protected by strangers?"

"It's not like that, Trace. It's—"

The gunshot burst through the air, birds taking flight in the melee.

Trace didn't think. Didn't question the instinct.

He threw himself at Nic, wrapping her in his arms and cushioning her with his body as they hit the ground.

Chapter 2

"Smooth moves, Romeo. I'm sure it's every woman's dream to lie buried in a patch of scrub grass."

His brother's amused voice floated over him as Trace rolled off Nicola with an alacrity he didn't know he possessed based on the way his head still throbbed.

"What the hell are you doing, Garner? And for the record, she wouldn't be lying in a pile of scrub grass if you weren't shooting at us."

"I wasn't shooting at you. I came to help."

Trace heard the subtle distinction in his brother's voice and ignored it. "Right."

He got to his feet and extended a hand to Nic. He saw her eye his fingers and guessed she was near to shaking him off before thinking better of their audience. It was only as her hand closed around his that Trace recognized his mistake.

Despite the cool air, her hand was smooth and soft and warm. Even better than how she felt was the way her fingers nestled beneath his, a perfect fit.

A remembered fit.

"You going to introduce me?"

Although Trace loved his brother beyond reason, at the moment he'd have been happy if the ground opened up and swallowed Garner whole. Not only was his little brother in the way, but he'd drunk as much the night before and appeared to be no worse for wear.

Perhaps because *little* was a poor description of the six-foot-three-inch former navy SEAL who could still bench three hundred and had shoulders roughly the size of a small truck.

Pissed at the situation and the odd hand fate had just dropped in his lap, Trace tilted his head toward Nic before firmly turning his back. "Nic Miles. My brother, Garner Withrow."

Garner moved up beside Nic as Trace headed off for Magnum, who even now stood about ten feet away. Despite the lack of a tether, the animal had remained in place. Out of boredom or some equine curiosity, Trace had no idea. But he counted himself fortunate he didn't have to add horse wrangling to the morning's adventure.

Especially with his brother's random gunshot.

Magnum had earned himself some extra sugar cubes for the equanimity and serious demonstration of his training.

What the horse couldn't manage, unfortunately, was figuring out how to pick up the pieces. Because while she still hadn't told him much in the way of usable information, Nic was scared. He'd seen her a lot of ways in a lot of situations, but this was a first. Add on a clear streak of maternal—or at least familial—concern, and something had her spooked.

And he was the one she'd hunted down for help.

Her comments suggested someone on the inside, but why now? Or maybe a better question was what had her spooked enough to suddenly take his advice to perpetually watch her back?

Again, all he could come up with was *why*.

Or perhaps a modified: *Why him?*

The day he walked out of CIA headquarters was also the last day he'd seen her. And he'd spent the past twenty-four months well aware he'd never see either again.

Yet she'd come for him. And remembered vacation story or not, she had to have done some digging to find him. He technically hadn't gone off the grid, but he knew how to bury himself deep, and old habits of self-preservation died hard. Even the horse training business he was building was shrouded deliberately in a corporate shell.

His new life was his choice, but he'd made a lot of choices in the old one that could haunt him if he wasn't careful. When he'd made the decision to start fresh in Liar's Gulch, it was to truly do just that.

Besides, he liked Liar's Gulch specifically because it was hard to find. And he'd further buried his personal information to avoid any visitors from his past. Since Garner had felt the same way after his last SEAL mission gone horribly wrong, their new situation suited them well.

Both of the Withrow brothers were well trained, with years of professional skills still honed sharp. Out here, they could build their equine business as they saw fit. Along with that work—if they decided to act—they could also choose the occasional job that utilized those still-sharp skills for the genuine betterment of others. *Mercenary* was a term with challenging overtones, but it was essentially what they'd become. Only instead of taking jobs for the pay, they each took jobs that provided a way to pay back a former sin.

Trace found missing people and dispatched relatives who regularly overstepped the bounds of what family should endure to far-off places. Garner had taken a particular interest in cold cases, his tenacity and sheer stubbornness serving him well.

And the best part of it all was that each job came with a discreet referral from someone they trusted. Trace's time in the CIA and Garner's in the SEALs ensured they had a strong network of connections. Connections who'd proven themselves over time as determined to work on the right side of the law. As of this week, they'd become a trio when they added Garner's buddy from high school, Jake Stilton, into their midst. A former detective for the Las Vegas PD, Jake seemed happy enough with the decision to trade the Strip for this small corner of nowhere.

As happy as any of them could be anyway.

Jake's arrival had also coincided with the evening's questionable fun at the town bar.

Trace patted Magnum's neck before turning back to where his brother still stood by Nic. He'd overheard their polite conversation, which was an odd joke all its own since *polite* wasn't an adjective he'd use for either his brother or the woman who still haunted his dreams.

A fact his brother was aware of.

Garner might not know Nic by name, but he knew there'd been someone in the past. He'd stayed quiet about it, but Trace knew Garner knew. Another night like last evening, shortly after Garner had settled in Liar's Gulch, had brought on a degree of soul-searching and confessing Trace normally avoided like the plague.

Only that night the whiskey had loosened his tongue. Happy to see his brother again and happier that Garner had survived his last mission—a fate three of his fellow SEAL brothers didn't have—Trace had talked of the woman who nearly did him in.

A decade and a half as an elite operative hadn't been the thing to break him.

A woman had.

So yeah, he'd spilled his guts and given up the real reason he left DC. Why he'd given up the CIA. And why he was determined to live his life with minimal attachment, brotherly bonds the rare exception.

Only now she was here.

And his carefully constructed world had just gone down like a house of cards.

"So you're the brother," Nic murmured as she traipsed back along the rushing stream that led toward Trace's property. She'd checked the area out thoroughly, having already seen the entrance to the large property from the front when she drove by the day before. This morning had been the second part of the exploration, working her way through the hundreds of acres that backed the wide expanse and culminated in this small tributary of the Snake River.

She hadn't lied to Trace—she was desperate, and she was increasingly running out of time—but even with the ticking clock in her mind counting down over Olivia's head, Nic had known she had to be prepared to meet Trace head-on.

She was on his turf, and that required preparation and an understanding of what she was walking into.

But the brother, too?

"And you're the ex," Garner whispered back, his voice equally low.

He knew about her?

Whatever she might have anticipated, Trace sharing the details of his sex life wasn't on the list. The man was a vault, almost in the literal sense of the word. It was a challenge to get anything out of him, and she'd always counted herself lucky somehow whenever she gleaned a small nugget about him or his past.

He could carry a conversation, that was for sure. He was charming and oddly sweet, and it still galled her that it had taken her as long as it had to realize how smoothly he could talk about any number of subjects and still avoid saying anything of substance about himself.

The reference to his wilderness haven had been one of those rarities. And the talk of a brother late one night after a difficult mission had been another. The rest of what she actually knew about him beyond the physical could be ticked off on the remaining fingers of one hand.

"You going to tell him why you're really here?" Garner's voice remained low, but still loud enough she suspected Trace could pick up on it.

"I already did."

"And?"

"And what? Ball's in your brother's court now."

The muttered "the hell it is" that came winging back through the crisp morning air was the only sign he'd heard her.

But he had.

Garner fell silent, drifting away to make his own path back to the house. She was grateful for the reprieve and took in the surroundings as they walked, careful to look at the landscape and not at Trace's impressive shoulders and delectable backside. She was basically just reversing her early morning course, but she looked out over the landscape with fresh eyes.

Determined eyes.

Because there was no way they could remain on Trace

for any longer than necessary. Besides. She'd conquered the first hurdle. Trace hadn't actually shot her, nor she him.

Which was a relief.

Since the discovery Olivia had been taken three days ago, Nic had gone through any number of scenarios in her mind. The first day she'd spent tracking and tracing the child's whereabouts for the previous week. Although technically under federal protection, Olivia was being watched versus held in place. A reality Nic regretted now but which the child's mother had insisted upon.

No one in the Brigante family actually believed Olivia was in danger. And while the CIA had done their best to convince Eloisa Brigante, the child's mother, that her daughter was at risk from her brother's shadowy organization, the guidance was disregarded as laughable.

"My brother runs an import-export business." Eloisa held up a hand replete with gold rings, her perfect, pink-tipped nails waving in the air. "I realize that you government people often think that's code for any number of crimes, but it's not. Richie's been part of the family business thirty years, first working in it and now running it for almost two decades. He's a good man. The best. I would never put my daughter in harm's way."

"But, Ms. Brigante," Nic tried again. "We've intercepted several suspicious containers across three different ports. All shipments not noted in any manifest. Your daughter's computer abilities are cause for concern."

"Because she knows how to code?"

"Yes. That combined with her rather precocious attempts at interacting with government websites."

Interacting was a subtle euphemism and *precocious* actually translated to successful intrusion into three dif-

ferent government databases, which was the only reason
Nic had managed to secure an audience with the child's
mother. She had more than enough ammunition to make
life difficult for the kid, and the mother knew it.

But once her team had done some digging of their own,
they realized that a kid who helped the government's over-
worked computer geeks find and quickly patch holes was
worth her weight in gold.

She was also an in with Brigante Container Corporation, which was how Nic was brought in on the project.

Eloisa's perfectly plucked eyebrows slashed down.
"That was a misunderstanding, nothing more. And the
coding is for a project at the private school she goes to. All
that…" another wave of the hand "…STEM stuff. She's a
bright girl. That's all."

With the brick wall standing firm and high, Nic tried
another tack. "Allow us to watch out for her then. Our officers are discreet and will blend in."

Eloisa stared her up and down. "You'd blend in with
a bunch of kids?"

"We're trained for it."

Eloisa shook her head. "My kid'd make you in thirty
paces. So would the rest of them. They're sharp, and they
pay attention."

Nic heard the protest, but she also saw the discern-
ible edges of fear in the woman's dark eyes. Eloisa might
want to believe her brother was running an aboveboard
business, but that small skitter of fear suggested she did
have questions.

Nic considered how to play it, her mind whirling
through each approach before discarding several. Whatever else she was, Eloisa Brigante was clearly used to hiding that fear behind confident bravado. She wasn't going

to be swayed by a sympathetic ear. Nor was she going to be bullied into a decision over her child.

In the end, Nic went with the simplest answer. "Then it's up to me to make sure I blend in, and the kids don't make me or anyone on my team. It's a good thing I still fit into my high school uniform."

An approach that had worked until it didn't, Nic thought with no small measure of disgust as they crossed out of the woods ringing Trace's property and onto the grounds of what was clearly his living area. A rambling two-story farmhouse was visible about three hundred yards off, with land still stretching beyond it. A dirt road cut through the land, and in the far-off distance she could see a small quaint-looking log cabin.

Where Garner lived?

It would make sense. They might be brothers, but it would be difficult to combine lives under one roof at their ages. Nic made a mental note to ask before coming back to her senses and firmly striking it. She didn't care where or how Trace Withrow lived or who he lived with. She needed his help, and that was all.

Then she'd be gone.

And he'd go back to living whatever life it was he'd chosen up here in the Wyoming wilderness.

A large sturdy-looking stable sat off to the north of the main house, and Trace led his horse determinedly in that direction. Garner was already heading for the main house without a backward glance, his interest in what was going on either quelled or he was using that lack of concern as a ruse to get more dirt later.

Which left her to choose the lesser of two evils. Follow a stranger into the main house or follow a man she knew far too well into the stable?

As images of Olivia's cheeky little wave as she headed into school this past Friday filled the forefront of her thoughts—the last time Nic had seen her—she opted for the devil she knew.

And the one she'd come to for help.

Trace had felt her gaze hard and heavy on his back the entire walk back to the stables. He'd have preferred to ride Magnum, but even he wasn't such an ass that he'd leave Nic behind.

And stuck with his brother, no less.

"You really must need my help." He shot the comment back at her, damning himself by turning around.

She stood in the open doorway of the stable, early morning light haloing her in the frame. Something clenched hard and low in his gut.

Desire? Probably.

But even that was too simple for the swamp of feelings that hadn't let go of him since he turned around to find her staring at him down the barrel of her gun.

Unwilling to spend any longer with the ghosts of his past, he shifted his full attention back to his horse. He made quick work of Magnum's saddle and riding tack before providing the sugar cubes he'd already promised in his mind. The horse's lips feathered over his palm, the sugar gone in an instant before Magnum nuzzled his shoulder for more. The move was as affectionate as the horse got, but Trace took it for the genuine compliment that it was. Magnum's respect might be grudging in his own equine way, but it was absolute. Trace dug a few more cubes out of his pocket, more than grateful for the camaraderie.

As the sugar disappeared, Trace was satisfied he'd settled his immediate debt. He closed the horse's stall door and offered the promise of a return for a midday snack and some time with the currycomb.

He couldn't delay any longer.

Turning toward Nic, Trace was relieved she no longer stood in the doorway, the sunlight a halo over her blond hair. The woman wasn't an angel, and he'd do well to remember that, most recent imagery aside. She had moved fully into the stable, standing beside an empty stall door.

When he bought the property, he'd selected it specifically for the acreage and the ability to build out a proper stable facility. The existing structure had been small, and other than using it as a temporary space for his and Garner's mounts, he'd set about immediately working on the new state-of-the-art facility that he imagined for his program.

His focus was twofold: building a strong program that could both train horses from a young age as well as rehabilitate those that might not move into working ranches but could make wonderful horses for individuals. Since he'd finished out the stables the previous winter, the structure now housed Magnum, a pretty bay quarter horse Garner loved named Lucille, as well as six more that were swiftly moving through the program.

"This is quite a stable." Nic had moved closer, her attention focused on the large brown-and-white Appaloosa peeking over his stall in curiosity at the new visitor.

"It's the heart of my business. I'm determined to build the finest horse-training program in Wyoming."

It was oddly satisfying to see the surprise flash in her blue gaze. Nic had always known how to hold her emotions close, so that slip was as interesting as it was intriguing. "I thought—"

"I came up here to loaf around and play at ranching."

"No, of course not. I guess I just didn't realize you had such a thing for horses."

If asked even a few years earlier, Trace wouldn't have said he had a *thing for horses*, either, but the decision to leave the CIA and all he'd ever known had forced him to reconsider what he did want out of his life.

The animals were simple—real—and they provided a level of solace he'd never imagined. Along with the selective assignments he and Garner chose to take on, Trace had used the past two years to regain control of his life. It was hard-won, but it felt real and right and true, even as recently as his hungover ride out this morning.

Which made it such a shock that this woman had managed to upend the equilibrium he'd finely honed these past twenty-four months. A truth that hit him like a ton of bricks as Nicola Miles still stood fully in his line of sight.

"I am sorry about the gun," Nic added when he still hadn't responded, that crystalline gaze never leaving his. "I was pretty sure you'd help me, but I needed to hedge my bets."

"Sure. Right."

"And a kid's involved."

That was the second time she'd brought up the kid, and Trace wasn't sure what to make of it. While they'd spent precious little time together discussing future hopes and dreams, when they did discuss anything beyond their world at the CIA, it wasn't to talk about children. Did she want them?

And what was it about this one child in particular that had her so insistent?

Trace might have his own personal lingering issues with the CIA and how the agency operated, but he'd always taken his work seriously. He believed in what he was doing and took pride in the fact that their work ensured the safety of millions of people. But he'd learned early in his training that you didn't get attached to an asset. That way lay madness.

Not to mention a personal attachment could get you and the asset killed.

Nic knew that as well as he did. So what was going on here?

He didn't want this. Had actively left DC to avoid facing any of it ever again.

Yet as he stood there, staring at her, he knew the truth.

He was in. He had been since the moment he caught sight of her with that damn gun pointed at his chest.

It had never been anything else with her.

Whether he wanted it or not, Trace didn't need the details to know the truth. He was all in.

Chapter 3

Although she'd have preferred the more earthy air of the stables and the space to move around, in the end, Nic suggested they head into the house. Coffee and a computer were in order for what she needed to do, and both were in short supply out with the horses.

Soon, coffee, hot and black, was in a mug in front of her. Trace had a matched mug of his own as he took a seat opposite her in the kitchen. "What's the CIA doing playing bodyguard to a kid? On US soil, no less."

Right to the point.

Which was what Nic needed, not to mention the reason she was here. But would it kill him to ask a few pleasantries first? How was she doing? Was that bistro they loved in Georgetown still open? Who's running the department now?

With that uncanny knack he'd always had, Trace eyed her over the rim of his mug. "And does Mick's still serve that mussels-in-garlic appetizer I loved?"

"I don't know. I haven't been ba—" Nic hated the prim tone. Hated even more that he'd read her so easily. "I haven't been there in a while."

He shrugged, but she saw the first semblance of a smile at the corner of his lips. "I'll have to look up the menu on-line." The smile vanished, falling away quickly enough. "Now. Walk me through it."

"The CIA's been following the Brigante family's activities for a few years now."

"Brigante?" Trace's eyebrows rose. "Shipping?"

His question was proof that she'd come to the right place. He might believe himself long past his time in the CIA, but it was clear he was still on the pulse of, well, everything.

"The owner hit the radar the first time a shipment came up short versus its manifest, and we've been keeping tabs ever since."

"What does the kid have to do with it?"

"Niece to said shipping owner. Genius IQ. And a special sort of skill with the computer."

Trace sat back at that and stared down into his coffee. "You think the kid's helping?"

"I think the kid's being forced to help. And because of those superior skills, she's been kidnapped by the uncle. Her mother wouldn't let us put her under protection, and other than a lot of suspicion we don't have anything to make the situation a more formal arrangement."

"So why are you pushing this without proof?"

"Because I know. I recognize the kid's skill and vulnerability. She's at risk, Trace. And now that she's gone missing, it's on me that I didn't push the issue and follow the instincts that have been clamoring about this from the first."

"What do you have on the uncle?"

She enumerated the list of details they'd secured over the past few months: the continued gaps in the manifests each time a Brigante freighter came into port; the suspicious loss at sea of a ship bound for the Middle East; and a strange run-in with pirates in the South China Sea that had the air of a faked tragedy stamped all over it.

Trace listened to it all, taking it in and saying little. Yet as Nic watched him, she saw what she always had: the way thoughts and ideas moved through his mind. Saw the way a plan built and evolved and came together as he listened to her.

It was only when she was done that he finally spoke.

"And you say the mother's firm that her brother's clean and the kid isn't in danger."

"Yes."

"Any reason to think the mom's involved? Or worse, the kid?"

Nic set her mug down. The thought was the logical next step—it was what they'd trained for—and the speed with which he'd arrived at the conclusion was one thing. The fact that it matched her thoughts as she'd worked this case, even more so.

She'd dug hard into the mother, especially after Eloisa seemed so reluctant to have her child placed under protection. And from the start, Nic had looked every which way she could think of against Olivia. It went against every instinct to think a kid was capable at that level, but she'd learned long ago not to assume. Or to underestimate the power and skill of a child. Especially at fifteen.

Although she was now twice that age, Nic still remembered that time. Remembered how clearly she saw the world and her role in it. And could recall, with absolute ease, how determined she was to make the life she wanted.

For her, that was the CIA.

It wouldn't be a huge leap to assume Olivia could be recruited into the family business. Especially if the computer work gave her a chance to flex muscles she was already proud of. In control of.

"Any chance the kid just went under for a few days? Played hooky on Friday and laid low for the weekend? Does she have a boyfriend? Girlfriend? Secret passion project?" Trace listed off the possibilities, and Nic recognized the validity in walking through all of them again with fresh eyes.

Even though she'd discarded each and every one already.

"Nope. None of those things."

He got up to refill his mug, crossing back over to her to give her a top-up as well. "Looks like you've got a missing asset then."

"And?"

"And it looks like I'm going to help you find her."

Trace was still cursing himself an hour later as Nic flipped through various files on her computer. Although he'd known damn well that he was going to say yes about eight nanoseconds after she asked him for help, he'd envisioned himself playing it a bit cooler. Probing for more details. Pressing her on what work they'd done to date to protect the kid.

Hell, even just sitting there with his resting jerk face to make her sweat for a few minutes.

But damn it all, there was a kid involved. A smart kid who had to be scared out of her mind if she was being held by someone she would have trusted. It was the vulnerability that tugged at him. That lack of power that defined childhood. It had certainly defined him and Garner and, from what he'd pieced together in their time with each other, Nic as well.

Nic tapped a few keystrokes, screen after screen lighting up with information as she walked him through the case file. The tech she'd logged in to was impressive. He'd been gone two years, but in that time the security had advanced several generations. Her log-in from a SAT phone had followed with an extensive VPN protocol that would make a tech geek weep.

But once she got through… Hoo boy, it was the mother lode.

"Is there any file you can't access there?"

"No."

They were sitting side by side at the kitchen table, and just the way she tilted her head to look at him nearly had his breath catching in his throat.

How could he have forgotten how beautiful she was?

Her beauty had always been something that could stop him in his tracks, and he was suddenly grateful for the firm chair beneath him. She wasn't classically beautiful. Her features were too sharp for what would technically pass as physical perfection. Yet there was something about the way all those angles fit together, set off by a soft sweep of hair that framed her chin, that had done him in from the first.

From the moment he met her, he'd longed to touch all those hard angles and explore what he just knew would be soft skin beneath his fingers. Those sharp edges had always suggested a man should back off, yet all he'd wanted to do was move in close.

And he hadn't been alone in his attraction. They'd worked together for nearly a year before they'd given in. Before those three glorious months when she was his. Through the ups and downs of their job. Through the nights that never stayed dark quite long enough to satisfy his need for her. And through the moments—far too few of them in the end—when he'd felt himself giving in to something that was bigger than he was.

A need so fierce and deep that it had scared him beyond measure.

Guns and criminals and the world's safety hanging in the balance…he'd trained for that.

But love with an equal? Nothing could be harder. And, in the end, impossible.

"Flip back to the page on the uncle."

She did as he asked, the dossier on Richie Brigante filling the screen. Trace was grateful for the distraction and turned his attention to the always-thorough briefing document.

The guy was in his late forties and had been involved with Brigante Container Corporation since high school. Despite it being a family business, young Richie had needed to earn his keep along with the rest of the staff that worked there.

Trace scanned further, noting the guy had done it all. He'd filed paperwork in the home office, done a six-month rotation in the shipping yard and then followed it up with three rotations at sea. Far-flung places, too, with real challenges to cargo ships, not some rich-kid pleasure cruise down to the Caribbean. The man was trained in the family business from the ground up.

"What about the mother?"

Before Nic could do it, Trace was following the thought with action. His hand brushed over hers as he reached for the keyboard, and he felt the warmth of her fingers where they brushed his.

It was a stupid accident, but he felt the touch echo more

keenly through his body than any physical encounter he'd had in the past two years.

And he didn't miss how she snatched her hand back as if singed.

He ignored it, already feeling stupid for the well of emotion he wasn't able to hold back and hadn't yet figured out a way to ignore. The coffee had kicked in and, along with three aspirin, was holding the headache at bay, but the rush of seeing her again was still too close to the surface.

He needed to get control.

And there was no better way to do that than to bury himself in work.

He was free at the moment, his last job having wrapped a week ago and nothing new on the horizon. What was likely going to be another week of fishing, working with the horses and doing some cleanup around the ranch wasn't meant to be.

They had a kid to find.

Trace toggled up and down the page with the arrow keys, reading the dossier on Eloisa Brigante. She'd married the kid's father briefly around the time she got pregnant but had kept her maiden name.

"Didn't want to give up the prestige of the family moniker," Trace muttered. Even as he thought it, he recognized that the kid had the name, too. "That's interesting."

"What?"

"The mother did marry the father but kept her own name. Big money and lots of influence, that makes sense. But she gave the kid the same last name."

"Rich people do strange things."

"Sure." They did do strange things, and Trace had been around long enough to know there was no accounting for any number of human quirks, but it still struck him as a bit…off. "Didn't the father have a say in it?"

"We looked at him early on. Nothing much popped. He visits Olivia for birthdays and holidays, and that's about it."

"So not involved in supersmart kiddo's life."

"Maybe it works for them."

He caught the edge of something in her voice, and curiosity tugged at him. "Maybe it does. Or maybe it doesn't."

"You think the father's involved?" Nic asked.

He shifted his attention off the screen, careful to keep his expression neutral. "I think I'm asking."

She sighed but eased off a bit. "All I mean is that I've already looked under that rock. Just like I looked at extended family, friends, any other rich kids' families she goes to school with. Sometimes kids just get a crappy family deal."

He almost believed her. The nonchalant way she went through the list. The idea that she'd turned over every stone. But it was there at the end, when she mentioned that oh-so-true reality of childhood for some, that he saw it.

Crystal fire.

It lit the depths of her blue eyes, flashing like a lightning storm, and added even more proof that something about this job had become personal for her.

"Okay, fine. Maybe it's not the father. But maybe it turns right back to Olivia. What if the kid resents the crappy family deal? And what if the crappy family deal makes her even more willing to help the uncle?"

"That's an awful big leap, Trace."

"Is it? Childhood experiences, especially trauma, can drive a hell of a lot of bad decisions." They'd certainly driven his life.

But this wasn't about him. A fact that was increasingly clear as he watched the emotions play across her normally stoic face.

Nicola Miles was a highly trained agent of the government. She knew how to assess any situation and adapt. And she never let her own emotions come through.

So why now?

And why this case?

That lone question continued to hammer at him. Yes, she saw something in the kid. Even if it was something kindred, the fact remained Nic knew how to keep her professional priorities intact. Always. Hadn't he learned that the hard way?

She was the consummate professional, and she never let her emotions interfere with…

"Well, hell." He spit out the words along with a few more choice curses as the truth sank in. She'd even told him herself, yet he'd blithely ignored whatever problems she was battling inside the organization. "Who's involved in this?"

"No one. I mean, I can't prove—"

"Nic." He let her name hang there, unwilling to give another inch. Damn it, not even another millimeter.

"I—" She stopped, the most indecisive he'd ever seen her.

And that was when the last puzzle piece fell into place. Nic, the ever-steady champion of the CIA, had well and truly had her blinders torn off.

"Who betrayed you on this?"

"I don't know."

"Don't know? Or won't tell me?"

Once more, something flickered in the depth of those eyes that were so good at shutting everyone out. Recognition? Or even just her own suspicions? "I don't know, Trace. But I know it's someone inside. They made sure the agents on duty on Friday were called off the scent for a matter of minutes. And in that time Olivia vanished."

Images of his life before flooded his mind. Trace had always known—or maybe more to the point, accepted— that the CIA operated under its own rules. Along with every other aspect of intelligence, there was no other way to manage the shadowy world that existed around infor- mation gathering, spy tactics and covert operations.

Anyone who believed otherwise was fooling them- selves. Hard.

Nic had always claimed she understood that, yet be- lieved in the underlying purpose of what she was doing. She believed in the men and women she worked with to achieve a common set of goals. And she believed that in the end the organization would always do what was right.

Not *easy*, she'd argued with him the few times their differing beliefs blew up into a full-out fight. But *right*.

"So you don't think she's with the uncle at all? You think the CIA's got someone kidnapping kids?"

"I'm assuming she is with the uncle. But that one of our agents let him have her."

Sure, money was a powerful lure. And Brigante was wealthy, but enough for an agent to ruin their career over? Enough to put a kid in jeopardy?

Something didn't add up, and he was about to press her when the screen flickered, grabbing his attention. What he'd assumed was the screen fading to black as it went into energy-saving mode did the opposite.

"Nic? What is this?"

The gaze that had been tight on him flipped to the screen. "What's what?"

The dossier files onscreen faded to the background as a large terminal window popped up. It was the sort of window that came up before instructions to reboot kicked in. "What's it doing?"

The new window filled with code, the image at odds with the slick interface it replaced. This was rudimentary at best, and hardly a time for her computer to crap out on them.

"Should you restart—" The question died on his lips as words became visible in the command line.

Nic. It's me Olivia. I'm in trouble.

A cursor blinked at the end of the word *trouble*, like a flashing sign.

Are you there? You were just there. I saw you typing a few minutes ago.

"What does she mean she saw us typing?" Trace reached for the computer, but Nic beat him to it, tilting the machine toward her. A hard sigh whistled through her lips as she set her hands on the keyboard. Where are you?

The cursor barely had time to blink as Olivia's response came winging back. I don't know.

Who are you with?

I don't

The screen went blank, the code terminal winking out as if it had never been.

"What the hell was that?"

Nic tapped at keys, but no matter what she tried she couldn't seem to get the kid back.

"Can I try?"

She pushed the laptop toward him. "I think we need to act fast."

He wouldn't classify himself as highly proficient, but he'd had basic coding as part of his training. But after three attempts, he had to admit that he had no idea how to get the terminal back up onscreen. "The kid hacked a CIA VPN."

"I know."

Nic's words seemed to hang in the air between them before Trace pressed again, "A highly specialized, deeply veiled government database. And the kid hacked it."

"I know."

"Those are more than 'some skills,' Nic. That's a walking felony with a side of treason tossed in."

"I know!" She scrubbed a hand over her face before shoving her hair out of her eyes. "All right, Trace. I get it."

"What the hell are you involved with?"

"I'm not sure anymore."

Chapter 4

Why had she come here?

The question had drifted in and out of her mind throughout the long flights with three plane changes to Cheyenne. It grew more intense as she made the drive across the state to the barely-a-dot-on-the-map Liar's Gulch.

But it was nearly deafening earlier as she'd watched Trace walk around the stables, currying his horse, putting up tack and asking the pointed questions he was so good at.

It accompanied the other question that hadn't drifted far from her thoughts.

Who was this man?

She'd believed she knew him, but in the time since they'd been apart, Nic realized it was quite possible she hadn't known him at all. If she had, would she really have walked away?

Because that truth—the fact that *she'd* walked—had haunted her every moment of every minute they'd been apart these past two years.

Whatever she'd believed about their differences of opinion, she never doubted his competence or his inner drive. Neither had she ever doubted the core values and tenets he chose to live by.

He wasn't by the book, but he wasn't a villain, either. In fact, she'd increasingly come to admit he was one of the good guys. Maybe the very best.

Here in this completely foreign environment, he was calm, cool and competent. Just as he'd been in war-torn countries or in high-level tactical meetings in Washington, DC. And now he'd gone and done it again, those enigmatic gray eyes totally focused on her and the question of what had happened to Olivia Brigante.

"You owe me an answer."

She did owe him an answer, Nic admitted to herself. She owed him far more, if she were honest, but it was a place to start.

"I know. Truly, I do. But I can't say I know myself."

He sighed, but she saw a new level of acceptance in his gaze. It gave her the slightest shot of hope. And, maybe, a little voice whispered, proof she'd come to the right place.

He glanced at her dark laptop once more before nodding. "All right. Let's shift things a bit. You've got a missing kid and suspicious CIA behavior at the time the kid went missing. What else is off?"

"Off how?"

"This didn't just happen. You're a company man through and through."

She shot him a dark eye at that one. "Last time I checked, my equipment was fully female."

"Don't I know it." That gray of his eyes heated ever so slightly, and she wasn't dead enough inside not to register it. Was even more honest with herself to admit she'd have loved to see it flash a few seconds longer before he pressed on, "You know what I mean. 'Company man' isn't gender-specific but a type of agent. And you've been one since the day you walked in."

"As opposed to your shoot-first-ask-later renegade approach to it all?"

This time that grin flashed hard and long, and damn it if her breath didn't catch in her throat. "It worked for a long time. Until it didn't."

Since that smile was still firmly in place, Nic avoided going too far down the fanciful path her memories seemed determined to follow.

And then he made it a wee bit easier when he went straight back into interrogation mode, that smile falling only to be replaced with grim determination. "What else has been nagging your mind on this? Odd coincidences. Off moments. Strange flickers of awareness you can't shake. Something has to have your senses on high alert, or you wouldn't be so convinced this was an inside job."

"That's the problem. I can't point to anything specific. Nothing that I can clearly say is off. Yet it is. It all is."

"So someone's covering their tracks very well."

Was that it?

Before she could say anything, he pushed on, "You're on Rannell's team now, right?"

"How'd you know? You were gone before I moved over."

Trace shrugged, but the move was anything but casual. Did the man even do casual? She'd never seen it.

Instead, that laid-back veneer had always reminded her of a lion on the Serengeti, yawning one minute in the afternoon sun and then moving at warp speed toward a gazelle the next.

Nic had never considered herself a shy, retiring violet, but she'd also never been able to shake the mix of silent thrill and subtle admission that she was happy Trace Withrow was her ally, not her enemy.

"He's had his eye on you for a while. Figured he'd get his way sooner or later."

"Dirk Rannell is a highly respected member of the agency." One who'd first been a highly respected analyst who worked his way up the ladder into management. She'd always found him somewhat unconventional—the man's analytical talents were robust, but as a consequence he lived in his head. Still, he didn't suffer fools. Nor did he live so deeply in his head that he missed what was happening around him.

Despite all that, she liked working for him, thought him to be a fair man and often found the two of them simpatico on the analytical aspects of their work.

"Besides, it was a mutual move onto his team when you left, and Bane retired. Why do you ask?"

"Rannell's also a company man. Which leads me to believe he'd be hard-pressed to see some of his team members for who they were if you've got a snake in your midst."

"That's not very broad-minded of you."

"Yet I'm the one you came to for help."

The easy congeniality that had hovered between them even a few minutes before had faded, replaced by a simmering anger Nic recognized. Wasn't this how it always went down between them?

A big part of her knew she needed to keep her cool. She was on wickedly thin ice, after all. Especially with starting their reunion by pulling a gun on him.

But damn it all, why was he insistent on going straight back to jerk territory at the earliest sign of a difference of opinion?

"Before you start poking at me, would you give me a damn minute to follow you? You make assumptions about who I am, who I'm working for, why I'm here. You readily accuse others of having biases, but you refuse to see your own."

"You're right. And because of it, I got out."

Before she could respond to that, he was out of his chair, marching across the kitchen to a sleek coffee maker that looked like it could calculate the algorithms to put a man on the moon while it brewed a fresh cup.

Nic sat there a full thirty seconds, stunned.

Was he actually admitting he'd contributed to his exit from the CIA? Because whatever she'd thought about his departure two years ago, nothing would have made her think that decision was a mutual one.

"What's this about?" Nic asked, careful to keep her tone neutral.

"It's not about anything."

"Oh no. You don't get to do that. You don't get to drop bombs and then clam up like it's none of my business."

Whatever had immobilized her initially had her moving out of her chair, crossing to where he stood at the counter, his back still to her.

It dawned on her a heartbeat too late that she'd gotten too close. Heat radiated off that broad back in waves and she could practically feel the hard lines of his body beneath her fingertips, even if it had been twenty-four endlessly long months since she'd last touched him.

"It's not your business, Nic." The words were low. Feral. And tinged with a level of pain she'd never have imagined. Gone was that congenial man who grinned at her with a gleam in his eye that affirmed he'd seen her naked. In its place was a wounded animal. One who'd never fully healed.

So she reached out and placed her hand on that back, heat searing through her palm and radiating up her arm.

Only it was the wounded animal who turned on her, pain filling his gray eyes while a sense of isolation and loneliness she'd never seen before seemed to pulse in lockstep with that heat.

It was that moment when she admitted she'd overstepped.

Especially when his arms wrapped around her, pulling her close. Determination carved harsh lines in his face, and she had the briefest thought he looked like a fallen angel.

And then his head bent toward her, his lips so close they brushed hers when he finally spoke.

"What do you want, Nicola? Because I'm losing my patience waiting for you to answer my questions."

He was beyond this.

He *should* be beyond this.

He *needed* to be beyond this.

Yet less than an hour in her company, and all he could think of was getting his hands on this woman and touching all the places he knew ignited a blaze between them. And still, he held himself back, his lips hovering over hers.

"I want to find a lost child."

"Nope." He shook his head slightly, their breaths mingling. "That's too easy an answer. Try again."

"It's the only answer I've got."

He stepped back then, his body sending up flares to keep holding her while his will exerted a last fleeting attempt at saving himself. "Not buying it."

"You don't think this is about a child?"

He had to give her credit that she could manifest that

stern voice even when her breath was still ragged and her pupils were wide in those crystalline blue eyes. "I think you've convinced yourself it's only about a child, and we both know that's a lie."

"Her safety is essential."

"Without question. And I've already told you, I'll help you. What I want to know is why the first time you decided to run from your ivory federal tower you headed straight for me?"

"Looks like I'm not the only one running. In a span of ninety seconds, you've tried to change the subject, kiss me and twist the conversation back at me. What are *you* running from, Trace?"

He'd spent the past two years determinedly convincing himself he hadn't run from anything. That his time in the CIA was simply over, a tenure that ended when enough was enough.

Even if *enough* was finding out your boss and team leader had funneled secrets overseas to one of the worst terrorist groups in the world.

And even when *worse than enough* was when you took the intel to upper management who affirmed in no uncertain terms, yet without *actually* confirming a damn thing, that they'd sanctioned it.

All the memories mixed in with those truths swirled around the ones of him and Nic at the same time. Their liaison had started as a way to blow off steam out on missions and had turned too quickly into something more.

In the end, he'd accepted it meant more to him than it did to her, but he'd still have bet his last breath she'd felt the *more*, too.

"It was another time and place, more than two thousand miles from here," he said. "It's over and past."

"Yeah, right. If it's so over, why do you live up here so far away from civilization? And if your time in DC is so over, why can't you just respond to my questions?"

"Because I don't owe you answers anymore."

Without knowing why, Trace pushed off the counter and headed out of the kitchen without a backward glance.

It put him at a disadvantage, leaving when the conversation went dark and twisty, his parting shot bordering on petulant, but he couldn't stand there any longer. Couldn't stand there with his still-pounding head and the endless swaths of memories that wouldn't abate.

Most of all, he couldn't stand there with the gentle heat of her body and the scent that was distinctly Nicola Miles washing over him.

She'd still be there whether or not he escaped to tend the horses for a while. The kid would still be missing, too. And, damn it to hell, two years of secrets he wasn't able to face yet would still carve a chasm between them.

Each of those facts blazed through his mind as he stomped back into the stables five minutes later. He changed into work boots and set about mucking stalls, spending some quiet time with each of their equine charges and doing his level best to calm himself right out of his miserable memories.

It nearly worked until Garner breezed in an hour later. "There's an incredibly attractive woman working on a computer in our kitchen."

"Her prerogative."

Dark brows over deep brown eyes so like their mother's shot up into his brother's forehead. "You sure about that?"

"Don't you have somewhere to be?"

"Nope."

"I thought you were going to show Jake around a bit."

"He's still sleeping off his warm welcome into town last night."

Sleeping? Trace was about to think less of their new tenant when he glanced down at his watch only to realize it still wasn't even ten in the morning.

A fact Garner quickly punctuated with another reminder of last night's fun. "We didn't walk in until after two, and the guy spent nearly all day yesterday driving up from Vegas."

"Yeah. Right. Got it."

"Looks like you're stuck with me."

Trace narrowly avoided grunting at his brother before turning on his heel and heading down to Libby's stall. Their sweet girl—a black-and-white quarter horse they'd purchased the prior summer—leaned in to nuzzle his neck as he patted hers in turn. "How are you doing in this cold weather, baby girl?"

He moved into her stall, checking her water as he kept up a steady stream of nonsense about the expected snowstorm predicted for later that week and how they'd take good care of her through it all.

Despite his pointed attempt to ignore his brother, the man obviously missed the memo. "Those storm predictions sound like they're no joke."

Trace glanced up to find Garner's large form hulking in the doorway of Libby's stall. "It's snowed before, it'll snow again. We'll work through it."

"I suppose *we* will. But you and Nicola might need to travel in it."

Trace leaned on the broom he was using to clean Libby's stall and stared at his brother. "Why are you poking at this?"

"Consider this volunteering myself for service."

"Service for what?"

"Helping you get your head out of your ass. A state you'd better figure out pretty damn quick if you mean to actually help her."

The expletive hovered there, just at the edge of Trace's tongue. It nearly slipped out—he and Garner didn't exactly tiptoe around each other—but something held him back. And before he could think better of it, something even more uncomfortable fell from his lips. "You think I can't handle this?"

"I don't question your ability to handle things, Trace. I never have. What I question is your ability to come back from this."

Although they'd spent nearly their entire adult lives apart until Garner's move to Wyoming almost two years before, there was no one Trace respected more. Even in the moments when he'd happily punch his brother in the face.

"I know how to take care of myself."

"Something I never question. But your only focus in this will be taking care of her, and that's the real danger."

Trace heard something just beneath that answer—an honesty even more raw than Garner's words. "You don't like Nic."

"It's not that simple."

"You sure?"

Garner sighed and stepped backward through the stall door. "You keep leaping to answers that aren't mine. Why don't you finish up what you're doing, and we'll talk later?"

There were endless dimensions to their relationship— both steeped in being siblings *and* government operatives— but nowhere before had either of them ever used those things as an excuse not to hash out a problem.

The anger was already washing over Trace in a tsunami

at the idea Garner would walk away when stark reality slammed into it with the force of an earthquake.

Neither of them *ever* walked away.

Yet Garner was now.

Avoiding the urge to toss the heavy broom across Libby's stall, Trace lightly settled it against the far wall. Refusing to allow a single bit of that anger to reflect at her, he gave the horse a small pat and a few murmured words before gently closing and locking the stall door.

And then he went on the attack.

"I'm finished!" Trace hollered at his brother's retreating back.

"Later!"

"Sonofabitch," he muttered, chasing off after Garner. His head still throbbed with the hangover, and his emotions still roiled at Nic's return, and despite it all, Trace forced himself to remain in control.

Barely.

"What the hell is this all about?" He reached Garner just before he could cross the threshold of the barn.

His brother turned, but where Trace expected a matched wall of anger, all he saw was quiet resignation. And how was it *that* sparked more of his anger than actually locking horns like two angry bulls?

"You tell me."

"Oh, cut the cryptic BS, G. What is with you?"

The easygoing smile that normally filled Garner's face was nowhere in sight. Instead, all Trace saw was a grim sort of resolve. "What's the end game here?"

"I help Nic, and we save a child in grave danger."

"I don't doubt you'll do that. I mean after you save the kid. The real end game. When the mission is over, and you're finally forced to deal with having Nic back in your life."

"Why would I deal with anything? She's walking right back out the way she came in."

Garner's gaze never left his, even as his dark eyebrows slashed over narrowed eyes. "And you're gonna be okay with that?"

"Of course."

"Then you're telling yourself lies."

"I'm not—" Trace stopped and shook his head. He would not let his brother do this to him. He needed to keep himself mentally sharp and prepared, because no matter how much faith he had in himself and Nic that they'd bring the child home safely, it wasn't going to be a cakewalk. Wasn't that why Nic had come to him in the first place? "I can do whatever needs to be done."

"And you will do it. Being in love with the woman has nothing to do with that."

"I'm not in love with her."

"Then I'm forced to repeat myself." Garner's gaze only grew darker. "The end game matters a hell of a lot, and you're lying to yourself if you think otherwise."

Trace only stared at his brother, unwilling to ask the unspoken *why*. Even when Garner's unrelenting honesty continued unabated.

"Because you are in love with her, and I don't think you have it in you to watch her walk away twice."

Nic stared at her laptop screen, frustrated when each and every programming trick she possessed—though limited— failed to produce another connection with Olivia.

She could call in a favor and ask one of her tech geeks to help her, but she had no way of knowing where loyalties were held right now. She wasn't taking help off the table, but she'd been in Wyoming less than twelve hours. She'd like to give it a bit more time before tapping back into home base for help when the problems in Langley were the exact reason she'd left.

A raspy cough pulled her out of her musings when she looked up to find a tall, lean man with a few days' scruff, no shirt and jeans come strolling into the kitchen, a German shepherd by his side.

"Hello?"

He looked startled as steel blue eyes, shot through with red, met hers. The dog, on the other hand, seemed unaffected as he stared at her with big brown eyes, his stance perfectly still beside the man. "Hey." Before she could say anything, he added, "I'm sorry. I didn't know... I mean, I didn't realize—" He broke off, confusion adding to the mix of an obvious hangover. "Did you come home with me?"

"No."

"With Trace or Garner?"

"No."

"That's a relief."

He turned toward the counter and the coffeepot without a backward glance, and Nic was amused despite the odd greeting and obvious lack of memory from the night before. She normally wouldn't be quite so forgiving of such an oblivious reaction to sex with a stranger, but there was something about the guy that tugged at her.

A strange loneliness blanketed him—which was an exceptionally odd reaction to a total stranger—but the sense rolling off him was overwhelmingly clear.

Or at least it was to her.

"Is that how you greet all your one-night stands?"

The man never turned around, his words gravelly as he remained facing the coffeepot. "I've never been a big fan of them, so I couldn't quite say."

After a hearty gulp of what had to be scalding coffee, the man busied himself filling a bowl beside the fridge with fresh water and a second bowl with kibble he pulled from under the sink.

With the dog happily scarfing down his food—after the command that he could, of course—a few minutes later, the man finally took a seat opposite her at the table, extending a hand. "Jake Stilton." He nodded a head toward the dog. "That's Hogan."

"I'm Nic."

"How'd you wander in here?"

"I used to work with Trace."

Jake's gaze narrowed, and for the first time she had the subtle sense the dazed-and-confused routine might all be a bit of an act. "Man's a horse trainer now."

"I know."

"Do you?" Jake stared at her over the top of his mug that still puffed steam, and she couldn't deny the continued concern that he was burning a path down his esophagus.

She also couldn't deny the obvious questions of why she was here and what sort of problems she'd brought to Trace's doorstep.

Before she could summon up a response, Trace and Garner came into the kitchen. When she'd first settled herself at the large rectangular table, she'd thought the room rather expansive, but the space suddenly felt small with three large men and a dangerous-looking dog that had just finished its breakfast.

"Jake." Trace's voice held a raw edge she recognized. She'd heard it rarely in the time they worked together, but those ragged edges suggested he was keeping his patience on a very short leash.

"Morning." Jake nodded.

"I see you've met Nicola."

"Just sat down. We were getting acquainted." The wry tilt that edged Jake's mouth almost had her smiling in return, but Nic wasn't ready to poke the bear that was Trace Withrow in this moment.

Even if he had gotten all up in her space, then left her for an hour in the kitchen alone to reflect on...*easier* times between them.

"Yes, we were. Jake was unduly concerned I might have been a one-night stand who was overstaying her welcome." She added a syrupy sweet smile for good measure, only to get a wicked smile in return from the half-naked man across the table.

"A man can't be too sure when a pretty woman looking fresh as a daisy is sitting in his still-unfamiliar kitchen."

"Nic and Trace used to work together." Garner reiterated the path she'd already started down, before jerking a thumb over his shoulder. "Why don't we leave them to it since it looks like they're going to be working together again?"

Jake's steely gaze flashed with interest, but he stood and headed for the coffeepot. "Anyone need a refill?"

Trace's "no" came as fast as her own.

Which left Jake to offer up one more of those knowing smiles before he headed out, whistling for the dog. "Come on, Hogan. Let's go explore our new home."

Garner followed, giving the dog a wide berth, but Nic didn't miss the last glance he gave his brother before leaving the room.

Trace remained standing but did settle himself against the counter. "I see you met Jake."

"Another musketeer?"

"Maybe yes, maybe no. He's Garner's friend from way back. He's giving Liar's Gulch a try."

"I'd say best of luck to him, but he's not going to get very far unless he exorcises those ghosts in his eyes."

"That's an awfully quick take."

"One I'm well trained to make."

The mulish expression never left Trace's face, his mouth a grim line beneath the day's growth of beard. He did, however, back off a tiny bit as he pushed off the counter and crossed to the table. "Did Olivia reach back out?"

"No, and I haven't found a way to reverse whatever it was that she did to get into my system."

"Kid's smart."

"The kid is off the charts in every way. That's what worries me."

Whatever tension had gripped them from the start faded as Trace leaned into the case. "Isn't that a good thing?"

"Yes and no."

"If she's with family, that has to give her some protection. It's not an ideal situation, and we'll get her out, but do you really think her uncle's going to hurt her?"

Nic had weighed this problem since the moment she learned Olivia had been taken. It had consumed her all the way to Wyoming. The wild card in all this was Olivia. She was in danger *because* of how smart she was. "A child with such formidable abilities? That's what worries me the most."

"Her ability to use those smarts has gotten her this far," Trace said.

"And it's her lack of understanding of how to wield them that's put her in grave danger."

Chapter 5

Trace carefully folded the stack of laundry on his bed and cycled through all he'd learned that morning. His former colleagues had really fouled up the mission if they let a kid under their protection go missing. Ops weren't foolproof, but mistakes like this didn't rest easy on a team.

It certainly didn't rest easy on Nic. But more than that, there was a huge risk of embarrassment and head rolls for the higher-ups for a screwup like this.

His own experience there at the end had Trace considering if the loss of the child was deliberate. It couldn't be ruled out, but it did make him wonder if it was also a sign of more dysfunction in the organization than anyone wanted to admit.

When the world's a dumpster fire, you fight the biggest ones first.

Those prophetic words—offered by his first mentor once he'd joined the agency—drifted through his mind as he stowed his clothes in his dresser.

He wasn't immune to the global challenges faced by everyone in law enforcement, no matter the level or jurisdiction. The work was hard. For a long time, he'd believed it was supposed to be hard. That was how he knew he was making a difference.

It was only when he understood the lines between good and bad were blurrier than he ever could have imagined that he'd given in and jumped ship.

What I question is your ability to come back from this...

The end game matters a hell of a lot, and you're lying to yourself if you think otherwise...

Because you are in love with her, and I don't think you have it in you to watch her walk away twice...

Trace shook off Garner's words, unwilling to think of them as anything but his brother's overactive protection gene kicking into high gear. He knew his own damn mind, and he'd done just fine protecting himself for nearly four decades. He didn't need platitudes or questions, no matter how well-meaning.

Which would have been fine, Trace considered as he dropped down on the bed, bending forward to put his head in his hands, if Garner wasn't right.

He *was* in love with Nic.

Hopelessly.

Desperately.

Two truths that flew in the face of every act of self-preservation he'd attempted.

Images he'd ruthlessly refused purchase in his mind's eye these past few years filled him on a rush.

The two of them laughing together over a bottle of wine at a sidewalk café in Paris the night they recovered nuclear codes put at risk by a double agent.

The hot, thick air that surrounded them on a mission in Colombia in the middle of August. The languid heat had only added to his need for her as they'd come together over and over in their small hotel room.

And that last time together, in his bedroom in DC.

Their lovemaking had carried an urgency he'd never experienced in his life.

It had held anger, too, Trace admitted to himself as he stood up from the bed. Anger that carried him out of the city and more than two thousand miles across the country to live practically off the grid. Oh, he wasn't quite ready to make himself invisible, but he'd done a damn good job of locking down the essentials.

"And she found you anyway," he muttered to himself. A reality that wasn't going to change by hiding in his room.

A few minutes later, Trace walked back into the kitchen, only to find her closed laptop on the table. He supposed that act sent a bit of a message. The woman he knew wouldn't be parted from her work tech for any reason. The fact she'd left it there on the table had to mean that while she might be in Wyoming grudgingly, she did trust them.

It did leave him curious, though…

Where had she gone?

He hadn't seen a car when they walked back to the house from their initial meeting in the woods, and she had to be staying somewhere.

Snagging his winter jacket from the old coatrack near the back door, he headed outside. The driveway looked the same as earlier, Jake's truck still where he'd parked it yesterday when he arrived. Garner's SUV was visible through the open garage doors, and Trace's own was parked right beside it.

Where had she gone?

Even as he wondered, those heated thoughts from earlier in his room came winging back. For as intimate as those shared moments had been, he'd had no claim on her. Did he actually think he had one now? She didn't owe him her comings and goings. Nor did she need to check in.

But damn it, where was she?

The thought was punctuated by the sound of pinging gravel against steel, and a large black SUV came bumping down the long unpaved driveway.

The car looked like something they'd ridden in throughout their careers. *Large and in charge* was always how he'd thought of those enormous vehicles with their dark tinted windows and undeniable presence as they ate up the road.

But seeing her through the windshield now? Why did it tug at something he had no business feeling?

Because what should have given him the sense that she was in charge and prepared for anything, several tons of cool machinery under her perfectly formed ass, left him feeling differently now.

All he saw now was a woman alone.

Perched up there in the driver's seat, that cage of black steel around her, he saw vulnerability and a deep sense of loneliness as he looked at her. Maybe because he knew the truth. Reinforced metal and a large agency of professionals couldn't help her now. Nor would they save her if the mission went sideways.

It was all on the two of them to make this right.

Maybe it was because he recognized that look, staring back at him through the windshield. Had worn it himself for two long years.

There were moments it felt like a solid victory when it was you against the world. And there were others when you realized the bigger truth.

When the weight of it sat upon you.

Nic prided herself on thinking before leaping.

She'd learned early in foster care that a few extra

seconds to consider a situation before acting would pay dividends on the outcome.

Determine who was friend and who was foe.

Pick a fight and leap in, or stay the hell out.

Stay or run.

It was a philosophy that had kept her safe, out of trouble and, eventually, in a home with decent enough people who chose to truly care for her.

As an adult she was well aware that part of actually *being* a child was having impulses and acting on them like a kid would. Children weren't mini adults and expecting them to be lay the road to mindless frustration.

But it was her own deliberateness that had led to her career. A damn successful one.

Which made the image of Trace Withrow standing at the end of the driveway, looking at her through the big front window of the SUV, both unnerving and welcoming at the same time.

Trace was an impulse.

One of the few she'd ever given into and by far the biggest. He was also the biggest risk of her life. She still didn't understand if that was a good thing or a bad thing, but, well, she was here, wasn't she?

And they had work to do.

Hopping out of the vehicle, she slammed the door and walked deliberately toward him. "I left this parked about a half a mile up in the woods."

"A convenient getaway vehicle if you needed to kidnap me out there on the trail?"

"Maybe." She shrugged but couldn't quite rise to the bait.

Especially because it was true. She'd come prepared for her conversation with him, and part of that had been the gun she'd carried on her person and the rope and ties she'd carried in the pack on her back. To be honest, she'd had no idea what she'd find catching him unawares, and she hadn't been willing to take chances.

It was only now, a few hours later, that she realized just how much she'd miscalculated. Because where she was expecting resistance, she'd gotten a heck of a lot of acceptance.

"It also gives us the needed comfort to go off searching for Olivia."

"In that?" Trace's gaze drifted toward the SUV before returning to her face.

Unyielding. The lone word drifted through her mind as that gray gaze held hers.

He'd always been solid and seemingly impenetrable, no matter how much she wanted to trip him up. But he simply *was*. This unmovable force that fascinated her as much as it confused her and kept her off-kilter. He'd done it professionally. And he'd managed it in their personal moments, too.

Oh, they'd always been on a level playing field sexually. She'd never have slept with him otherwise.

But all the rest of it?

As soon as their moments of intimacy were gone, Trace went right back to that place she couldn't touch. Or understand. Or break through. All those places where he refused to let her in or see the man beneath the undeniably capable veneer.

The unending frustration of that came out in a snappish tone at his question. "Why not in this?"

"Because it screams government agents."

"It's a rental."

"It plays to type. As does the low-rent, nondescript

motel you're likely staying in. So no, we're not going in that."

The superior tone chafed, but Nic refused to give in. This was part of their patter, and she was damned if she wanted to fall so easily back into old habits.

Old, deliciously warm habits…

Instead, she did a quick scan of the area, from the battered truck in the driveway to the open garage doors across the way. "I haven't checked in to a hotel yet. Besides, what do you think will be better?"

"We've got a work truck parked out on the other side of the stables. It'll be our best bet."

Her hands went up to her hips without her even thinking about it. "Sitting up high in a truck without tinted windows that likely can't hit fifty in under thirty seconds?"

"You wound me." Trace slapped a hand on his chest in mock horror before shaking his head. "As if I'd ever have such a piece of crap on my property."

"Let me see it."

Trace waved her on, and they circumnavigated the same building they'd walked into earlier. His body was large beside hers, his steps moderated to account for her slightly shorter strides.

He'd always done that. That subtle suggestion that he was aware of her and considerate of her even when he had no reason to be.

She was highly capable. Well trained.

And damn it, that subtle accommodation still managed to make her heart rumble happily in her chest.

As advertised, an old work truck was parked in the back, looking like it had seen more than a few Wyoming winters and far, far better days.

"Clearly we have a wildly different definition of the term 'piece of crap.'"

Without saying a word, Trace went straight to the driver side door and, after opening it, hit a button to pop the hood. Nodding toward her, he smiled. "Take a look."

Her training had covered any number of topics, and one of those included vehicle maintenance of all different types. Even without a single bit of it, she'd have recognized the very large, polished-to-a-gleam engine shining beneath that hood.

"Is she street legal?"

"Barely." He smiled, his grin nearly feral. "Garner and I both believe in owning top-notch equipment. Regardless of what it might look like on the outside."

"I stand corrected."

He shrugged. "I might have led the witness a bit with the work truck reference."

That frustrating hour at the kitchen table when she'd done her best to backtrack Olivia's hacks into her system had been painful and fruitless. And suddenly felt overwhelming.

"It won't do us a bit of good if we can't find her."

"She found you once. That's got to count for something."

"Unless someone caught her reaching out to me."

Trace's gaze narrowed at that as he came around to drop the hood back into place. "From all you've told me, she's smart. She's evaded detection this long."

"She's still a kid."

"I'm not suggesting otherwise. But she's also proven herself resourceful and downright sneaky."

It was an honest assessment. Realistically, she knew that. And still… "You talk like she's brought this on herself."

"Don't mistake my meaning. Those skills are keeping her alive."

"Because she's a bratty kid?"

"Because she's resourceful and clearly has the ability to look out for herself, despite being surrounded by adults who should stand for her no matter what."

Nic had no idea why she was pushing this. Worse, why she was so unable to get out of her head when it came to this case. The one that kept telling her she'd be too late to save an innocent child.

But it was his solemn promise that went a long way toward allaying that unending swirl that refused to settle.

Lips set in a grim line, Trace said, "Which is why we will."

Olivia Brigante tucked her computer under a pillow and switched over to the one her uncle had demanded she use when he picked her up the other day. He liked to think he indulged her with fun things to keep her occupied, and she played along so he wouldn't figure out what she was really doing when she tapped away on her own keyboard.

She knew enough that she could use the computer he gave her to hack wherever she wanted—he'd never know any better—but it felt safer to keep her work separate from whatever it was he needed.

And wow, he needed a lot.

He'd asked her to look into a few airline flights coming in and out of Canada. He'd also asked for a few maps of wilderness routes from Alaska into Canada, Canada into Montana and Canada into Idaho.

Nobody would tell her where they actually were right now, but Uncle Richie kept calling it a dude ranch. He'd also made some weird excuse when he took her phone, saying how the owners thought cell phones made kids rude and he didn't want them to think less of her.

She'd nearly staged a full-on revolt at that but something in his eyes stopped her. Something she'd never seen before.

Fear.

He also told her he'd let her talk to her mom and he'd bring it to her then. In the meantime she was working on what she needed to get quickly off her phone when she did have it again.

The big house was nice, but she didn't like the people who owned it. John and Jane Smith. They acted friendly, but Olivia didn't like the overbright smile from the wife since it didn't match her mean blue eyes. And her husband seemed really clueless, since he didn't see how her uncle Richie kept touching Jane and making eyes at her each time John's back was turned.

Her mother had told her to humor Uncle Richie and help him with whatever he asked on their *little adventure out west*, but Olivia wasn't buying any of it.

Especially because those jerks were on their phones all the time.

Did they really think she was that naive?

She knew the only reason she was here was because her mom wanted to go off on another trip with her boyfriend, Lyle. An old man—Eloisa called him that when he wasn't around—but she went with him because he had a lot of money.

She'd met him through Uncle Richie, and Olivia didn't like it when Lyle was around. He had a calm voice, but he oozed something that made her uncomfortable. Like the way she felt when she looked at the snake her science teacher kept in the back of the room in their biology class.

It was supposed to be a big secret her uncle was involved in a lot of bad stuff, but Olivia wasn't sure why they thought they were all so secretive about it. Mom always called him her "innocent little baby brother," but Olivia knew it was a front for excusing Uncle Richie's behavior.

A fact she'd innately understood but which she got more wise about after overhearing Uncle Richie's ex-wife yell about him a few Christmases ago.

"You think of no one but yourself! You and that damn business and finding ways to screw people. You're a miserable man-child!" Aunt Siobhan had yelled before stomping out of the room.

Her father had been gone since she was small, so Olivia had never seen grown-ups fight like that. She figured she'd have missed that fight, too, if she hadn't been hiding on the staircase in her aunt and uncle's big house in New Jersey. She was staying there for a few days while her mom got wined and dined in New York by her boyfriend before Lyle.

Her aunt had also yelled some stuff about shipments and running supplies, and it had made Olivia curious. So that night she'd done some digging, hacking into her uncle's computer from her own laptop up in her bedroom. He'd been stupid enough to use a simple password—Siobhan—and she'd gotten into his home server really fast.

Once in, Olivia had read about the "shipments" her aunt had talked about.

A few files from Africa and Asia that had information about shipping routes. Then she'd stumbled on some other stuff. Things that talked about bombs and guns and ammunition, and Olivia recognized quickly that things didn't match.

The stuff from Africa and Asia looked like regular things businesses shipped, from fabrics to ceramics to plastics. But the other stuff?

Olivia had slammed the laptop closed and shoved her computer under her pillow that time, too, scared at what she'd discovered. Because whatever her mother had said for years about her "little brother," Olivia sort of thought those files made it clear Uncle Richie was anything *but* innocent.

Which was why she'd reached out to Nic earlier today through the agent's database. Olivia liked knowing she could access her that way and had kept that capability in her back pocket. The government got really pissy when you hacked into their networks, but she wasn't doing it to steal secrets.

She needed help.

She thought she could handle it all, but this morning her uncle asked her to look into the local police chief. Olivia had done it over breakfast, giving him the information he needed before heading back up to her room. They promised to take her out to explore the ranch today with some horseback riding, and she'd gone up to get ready.

Only when she'd gotten back to her room, she looked out her window to see the police chief out in the driveway with her uncle and John. The officer had looked mad as they all yelled at each other, and she got a funny feeling in her stomach.

Why did Uncle Richie ask her to look that man up and then go out and fight with him?

And who were the man and woman who owned the house? Her uncle kept talking about being college friends with John and Jane and how they went way back, but he didn't know small things like how long they'd lived in the house or if they had kids. Two questions she'd asked at dinner the night before.

Jane had laughed off her questions, but those mean eyes had stayed on her face a bit too long, and Olivia hadn't asked any more questions.

But it had all made her think about what was really happening. Something she'd wondered since Richie and Siobhan's fight at Christmas but which got bigger after Olivia met Nic.

Nic had found her at school and introduced herself one day.

"You can get in trouble for talking to me without my mom around," Olivia had sassed when the pretty woman started talking to her. What she hadn't expected was the quick agreement.

"You're right. I can. And I don't want to make you uncomfortable. But I am worried about you."

"Why would you worry about me? You don't know me."

"I was a kid who didn't have anyone to worry about me. So as an adult, I decided to make sure other kids didn't have to go through the same thing. Which is why I'd like to talk to your mom, too."

Nic had been really nice and had been adamant with her mom that she wanted to protect Olivia from something. But her mom hadn't believed her.

Only, Nic had nice eyes. And she hadn't lied. She'd given Olivia some information, all of which Olivia had corroborated when she did her own digging.

Which made her mad at herself now because she'd thought about calling Nic when the trip came up but hadn't.

And now there were weird questions about going back and forth to Canada.

And the police chief yelling in the driveway with her uncle and John.

And Jane Smith with the mean eyes, nearly walking in on her and discovering her talking to Nic.

Olivia ran her fingertip over the edge of her computer, stuffed beneath her the pillow.

And wondered if she'd ever see her own bedroom again.

The truck had been a bit of a joke, Trace could admit to himself now, but it had opened up something between them, too.

He knew damn well his equipment would see them through. He refused to surround himself with anything less, and the retrofitted truck was one small example of all he and Garner had invested into the ranch.

But the opportunity to tease Nic a bit had been... Well, it had broken the ice.

Maybe it had also given him a chance to prove to her, in a small way, that he was *in* on this. That he was still the competent agent she'd known. That he was still able to see a mission through.

And that he was still the person she could trust.

Of all that had come between them before he left DC, that was the part that had hurt the most. There at the end, when she'd questioned *them* because she questioned him.

That moment when his disdain for the organization they worked for spilled over to how she felt about him.

He'd put his life in service to the government behind him when he left and moved to Liar's Gulch. And up until that morning, he'd even believed it was all in the past.

Which made it both surprise and challenge to realize how much of it was still far too close to the surface for comfort.

Was it the work and the potential for a new mission that had churned it up?

Or Nic?

Because you are in love with her, and I don't think you have it in you to watch her walk away twice...

He shook off Garner's words once more.

This wasn't about them. But if it ended up exorcising some of those lingering relationship demons, Trace would count himself lucky. Saving a child and giving himself some semblance of a future? Win-win.

Especially because those relationship demons were increasingly causing problems of late. Sure, he found companionship when he needed or wanted it. But it wasn't until recently that he'd realized just how infrequent that need actually was. Needs that came back awfully damn quick the moment he laid eyes once again on Nicola Miles.

"I do believe you mean that. Even without knowing her, I know you'll stand for her."

Nic's words drifted toward him on the cold breeze that had kicked up in the few minutes since he'd walked outside to find her.

"Why wouldn't I?"

"There were days I wondered if the work had taken that away from you."

He wanted to be suspicious of her sudden change in tone, but no matter how ruthlessly his gaze drifted over her face, he saw nothing but openness.

"Taken what?"

"That ability to stand for anything any longer."

It was a harsh statement and Trace wanted to be angry

about it. The man he was two years ago would have been. Only now…

"Why would you think that of me?" he finally asked.

"Because I'm afraid it's done that to me."

It wasn't rational, and he knew damn well he didn't have a right to offer her comfort any longer, but before he could stop himself, he was moving forward and pulling Nic into his arms.

She went willingly—and wasn't that a surprise?—her arms coming around his waist like tight bands.

Trace didn't want to be affected.

He didn't want to *feel* like this.

But as her body pressed against his, he recognized he needed this as much as she did.

"It's not supposed to be like this." Her lips moved against his chest, the sound absorbing into his jacket.

"Like what?"

"You're supposed to be a part of my past."

"Yeah, well, ghosts have a way of coming back to haunt those they're not finished with yet."

She shifted at that, the vivid blue of her eyes meeting his as her head lifted. "You're not finished with me?"

It was a stark moment of truth. One he'd avoided diligently for more than two years. "I thought I was."

"And now?"

"I guess I was wrong."

A soft nod had her head moving, her hair brushing against his jacket. "I guess I was, too."

"What are we going to do about it?"

"The job. That's all we can do."

As if to punctuate the point, her arms dropped from his waist, and she took a few steps back. It didn't escape him that she just caught herself on that last step back, the slightest wobble visible in her stance.

Good. He wasn't feeling all that steady himself, Trace admitted, and it was a hell of a lot easier to brush it off when it was mutual. When it was something they both had to deny.

Which made that heat in his chest—the initial spark that fired when he'd first laid eyes on her this morning and had built into a steady burn in the hours since—so fascinating.

Because she wasn't immune, either.

They could both talk about the job all they wanted—even use it to put a distance between them—but his memory of their time together was good.

Damn good.

And as he recalled, the two of them had done just fine multitasking between the work and their need for each other.

Chapter 6

Nic could still feel Trace's arms wrapped around her as she headed back into the house. Those moments in his arms had been her first easy breaths since Olivia disappeared, and she hadn't realized just how much she needed that sense of support. Of human contact.

Only now she'd gotten another taste of depending on him again, and it was dangerous to her well-being.

She needed to stay focused on finding a child and getting her to safety. *Not* on her own hormones.

Ghosts have a way of coming back to haunt those they're not finished with yet.

Where had that even come from?

That whole exchange between them had been like something out of a dream.

Nic had sworn to herself before coming to Wyoming that she would remain professional no matter how tense the moments with Trace might be, and yet here she was, barely a morning in his presence, and they were talking about ghosts and pasts and…and being *finished* with each other.

What was she supposed to do with all that?

Nothing, she thought as she stomped toward the kitchen table and snatched up her laptop. She wasn't going to do a damn thing about any of it.

Especially now that she had some distance and a chance to think away from the temptation of the circle of his arms.

That was the key to all this, she admitted to herself as she walked into the guest room Trace had said she should use and closed the door firmly behind her.

Keep moving.

Stay focused.

Don't forget the mission.

Finding Olivia Brigante and getting her back safely was all that mattered.

Although Nic had no hope of hacking her way backward to reach the child in the same way Olivia had found her earlier, those moments out in the driveway with Trace had given her an idea. It had been a whisper of a thought when he'd popped the hood on the work truck, but it had grown stronger in her mind with each foot of distance away from him.

Get under the hood.

Images of that truck engine, gleaming a shiny silver, flashed through her mind as she opened up her laptop and hunted through a few of her intake files.

"Where did they take you?" Nic barely realized she asked the question out loud as she searched through a series of files her team had put together.

The case they were building against Richie Brigante was complex and layered and had been going on for some time. There had been a tremendous amount of work before she ever came onto the case, and they'd acquired even more since she joined the team a little over nine months ago: shipping records; business filings; real estate holdings. All were legitimate, but they still painted a picture of a man with considerable wealth that didn't quite match his apparent earnings.

It had been that disparity that kept her hunting for where his real sources of income were coming from.

And it had also led her to the sister and her child.

She'd had to work for it, but she'd eventually gotten approval to put surveillance on Eloisa and Olivia. Eloisa had been a pretty easy sell to her manager, but she'd had to make a real case to monitor a minor.

But she had built it, step by careful step.

The child's intelligence. The amount of time she spent with the adults suspected of criminal behavior. And, most of all, the continued exposure to that world in much of her free time, especially when Eloisa dropped her child off for days at a stretch.

It had started as a surveillance exercise and had morphed quickly when the restless, unquenchable depths of Olivia's intelligence spilled over to Nic. Even now, Nic remembered those first moments meeting Olivia, the child's mix of intelligence and humor capturing something inside of her.

Reminding her of a time so long ago when she herself had watched the world with careful eyes and very big ideas.

I CAN SEE YOU.

Nic had blinked at the laptop nestled on her thighs where she was hunkered in the corner of the school cafeteria. A text window had popped up with those words, a cursor blinking at the end of them.

She'd started the job three days before, and while she was well aware kids noticed everything, most also had enough hormone-filled contempt to deliberately ignore her.

Which worked just fine for her.

Until then.

More words flashed on her screen.

YEAH, LADY. YOU. SITTING THERE IN THE CORNER.

Despite her training and preference to avoid getting made—even in a high school—Nic looked up, her gaze scanning the cafeteria. Only to find nothing out of the ordinary staring back at her.

Which made the pixie-size human who plopped down beside her, clad head to toe in black with a thick purple streak in her hair, more evidence that Nic was off her game.

"Who are you?" the pixie asked.

Nic stared at Olivia and considered how to play the moment. Her presence might be obvious, but she was more than confident she'd stayed off the radar in her surveillance efforts. This was hardly her first stakeout. "An adult."

"Yeah, there are lots of those around. Who are you specifically?"

"My name's Nic."

"I'm Olivia, but you already know that." Deep brown eyes twinkled with merriment. "You're watching me."

"I am not."

"Sure you are. I saw you outside of school yesterday and parked down the block the day before and in the bar of the restaurant my mom took me to last weekend in New York City. You were a blonde there in a black dress and really awesome heels."

"I—"

Olivia leaned closer. "Gotcha."

Nic hadn't felt this off her game since she was in her first year, on her first stakeout, and even then she had never felt quite so exposed.

Or, frankly, stupid.

"You're mistaken."

"Nah, I'm not. But you can play cloak-and-dagger if you want. I'll keep your secret."

Nic hadn't been a teenager in a very long time, but those years were still emblazoned in her mind as if etched in stone. The frustration that no one gave you enough credit. For anything. And the deep desire to get out and get on with it.

It went against protocol and everything she'd been taught, but in that moment Nic went with instinct. Something Trace said once had drifted through her mind a split second before she did.

The rules are all fine and dandy until they're not. Quit using them when they don't work anymore.

"Why do you think I need you to keep a secret?" Nic asked.

"Because you've got questions about me. About my family. If I'm honest, there are days I have questions about them, too."

It couldn't be this easy, Nic had thought at the time.

And it hadn't been.

For all her bravado and smarts, Olivia didn't let on that she knew much of anything about her uncle's business. Nic figured a child as aware and as smart as Olivia likely knew *something*, but not a single bit of intel suggested the kid was involved.

She was at risk, living in the orbit of adults engaging in bad behavior, but she'd spent her life there and hadn't been involved.

Until recently.

The child she'd spoken to that day in the cafeteria—deeply precocious and terrifyingly brilliant—wasn't involved in Richie Brigante's crimes.

She was now. Nic would bet her life on that. And it was all likely beyond Olivia's understanding.

And against her will.

It bothered him that the kid got in.

Trace wanted to ignore that fact—scared, precocious kid and all—but it still bothered him.

Olivia Brigante had hacked a government database and communicated with a federal officer. And she'd done it on *his* Wi-Fi.

When he and Garner had made the decision to settle in Liar's Gulch, it was with the full knowledge they both knew too much. Way too much.

They'd agreed that while neither of them were interested in shutting the world out, they knew enough about it—and had made enough enemies between them—that they wanted to set up some security protocols from the start.

The work truck was one example.

State-of-the-art technology was another.

And a series of security cameras was yet another.

They'd made an investment in these tools as a way to ensure they had a future. To ranch how they chose. To step in and help others as they chose. Most of all, to live as they chose.

It wasn't off the grid, but it was managing the grid in a way that ensured their privacy, safety and, more than anything else, an opportunity to put the past behind them.

Olivia's hacking experiment meant they weren't nearly as safe and secure as they thought.

Trace pulled up the security application on his laptop and ran a series of protocols, trying to determine where it all came from. The kid was likely smart enough to bounce a signal off of several locations to avoid detection, but...

Trace tapped in a few commands, that *but* lingering in his mind. She was looking for help, not trying to evade detection. Would she be quite so concerned with hiding her digital footprint? He typed in a few more commands, looking for any sort of breach or even physical hack into his systems.

And fell back into the plush leather of his office chair a few minutes later when he came up with a big fat lot of nothing.

"I'll bet you we're looking for the same thing." A voice emanated from his office doorway, and he looked up, surprised to realize that once again today, Nic had gotten the jump on him.

"Oh?"

"I've been tracing anything and everything I can find on Olivia and her family for the past hour."

"Find much?" Trace asked as he stood, gesturing Nic to one of the chairs opposite his desk.

"I don't think so, but I wanted to run something by you."

Since it wasn't a flat-out no, Trace sat down in his seat after Nic took one of the chairs. "What do you have?"

"I'm not wasting time thinking we can backtrack through her hack to find her. Instead, I'm going to focus on what I do know."

"You don't think you can find the breach?" That surprised him, especially knowing the phenomenal talent in the agency when it came to cybersecurity.

"I don't think I can find it with *my* skills." Nic's smile was more a soft tilt of the lips, but he caught her wry humor all the same. "And I'm not ready to call in anyone for backup. So I switched gears and focused on what I do know after watching the kid for a month, as well as keeping tabs on her family for the better part of a year."

As strategies went, it not only made sense, but it matched what Nic was very, very good at.

Trace had known her—or more, he'd known of her—for a few years before they got together. Her reputation was flawless when it came to understanding her targets. She saw someone's life in clear patterns—who they were, where they went, who they were related to—in ways he'd rarely seen in other agents.

Of course, people could be trained and those skills honed over time, but she had an innate sense of people and the details that made them tick.

"What do you know?"

"Although we have nothing but circumstantial evidence, Richie Brigante is running an illegal business. It's exceptionally well managed and maintained, but there are too many moving parts and slight inconsistencies for him to be clean."

Although he didn't doubt her, Trace was curious to know more. "Such as?"

"His shipping manifests don't match the inventory he carries. He's got contracts with ports that don't seem a direct match for his business and in locations that are even less specific to the goods he imports. And the business is just *bigger...*" she waved a hand for emphasis "...for lack of a better word, than it should be."

"And you think Olivia's involved?"

"I didn't at first. I thought she was in danger due to proximity and her skills, but I didn't think she had actual involvement. Until now."

"What changed?" Her cheeks took on a decided blush, and he was curious as to what caused the change. "Nic?"

"The kid made me."

"When?"

The pretty blush only deepened, and he couldn't deny how compelling she looked. It was a far cry from the kick-ass woman he knew her to be, but that touch of embarrassment flared something inside of him.

One more proof point that she wasn't unaffected by the world around her, no matter how cool and aloof she could play it.

"When I first started to follow her, after going through all the motions to get approval to track a minor. I was in character and in costume, fully disguised each time I followed her. And she made me, Trace."

What had been pure interest shifted inside of him, and he couldn't hold back the grin. "I'd have paid to see that."

"I bet you would. I even used my best dress and wig, and the kid knew it was me."

"The Morocco disguise?"

"Yep. It's one of my best because the wig hides portions of my face, and it was like she didn't miss a beat. Olivia saw right through it."

"Eidetic memory?" He smothered an urge to complain about the agency's psychologists. "Or whatever passes for the broader idea of it that doctors will actually believe."

"I think so. The kid's special. She's frighteningly observant. And she processes it all with a mix of computer-level accuracy and a funny sense of humor. She's—"

Again, Nic searched for the right words. "She's unique and odd and wonderful in the best of ways."

In all the time they were together, Trace had never seen her quite so caught up in a case. Even more than that, she was caught up in the kid, that much was clear.

Yet even as he acknowledged it, Trace couldn't see how it was unhealthy. Focused, yes. But there was a sweetness to it and a very real level of concern he couldn't help but key into.

"For the obvious intelligence, and I'm assuming if tested she'd hit genius, there's a high emotional quotient there, too."

"Yes!" Nic leaned forward, excited. "That's absolutely it. She's not caged by her intelligence. But I am concerned that Richie or someone in his organization has figured out a way to use her."

"Why the change? You said you don't think she was involved when you first started tailing her."

"Despite her quick ability to make me, she was discreet about it."

Trace was starting to get a picture in his mind, and it was considerably more sophisticated than he'd first imagined when Nic briefed him on the assignment that morning. No matter how intelligent, the behavior Nic was describing had a layer of maturity to match that was maybe harder to believe than the depths of the child's intelligence.

"Discreet how? Most adults would tell someone about that sort of intrusion into their life. She kept it to herself?"

Nic nodded, that subtle swing of her hair brushing the edge of her jaw. "The whole time. Even when I finally went to her mother and told her of our concerns, Olivia kept it to herself."

"So she has to sense something is going on with the adults around her," Trace pressed, a deepening sense of unease at the child's proximity to all this. "Which possibly puts her in more danger. They've likely underestimated her up to now, but if she demonstrates any sense of understanding of what they're doing, the risk to her safety increases exponentially."

"Her risk is with the uncle. Eloisa keeps coming up clean."

"You really buy that?"

Nic stilled, something a lot like grief clouding her sky blue eyes. "It's a mother's job to protect her child."

"Yes, it is."

She sighed, the sound barely a whisper in the room. "Yet we both know not every mother is wired that way."

On that point, Trace admitted to himself, they'd always agreed. "Better than most."

Better than most.

Trace's words still lingered between them, weighted with a level of meaning neither of them had ever delved into too deeply.

All part of why your relationship was so easy at the start and so hard by the end.

That small voice, the one that hadn't shut the hell up since she'd started on this journey out west, reared its head once more.

Nic wanted to ignore it.

If she wasn't so head over heels at being in Trace's company again, she might have even been successful at doing just that. But something about being with him, in his home, near his brother and his friend and their collective new life, had all of it coming back. All the memories and feelings she'd spent the better part of two years placing in an emotional box that she kept firmly closed.

Much to her horror, but oddly not her surprise, was how quickly the lock that kept it in place snapped, breaking wide-open.

And just how easy it was to bring it all back.

They'd fooled themselves at the start, before the physical aspects of their relationship had ever begun. Before the fights and disagreements. And well before she'd realized her heart was in way too deep.

The conversations they'd both believed to be shallow—a simple way to pass the time on stakeout—had held depths neither of them had been willing to admit. And it was talk of their childhood, on the occasions the subject came up, that had been the deepest.

She'd shared her time in foster care and the changes in her life once she'd found her home with Jack and Lucy Baker. He shared—always in light anecdotes—how he and Garner had fended for themselves when his mother wasn't around. It was always the mother, Nic remembered, with no mention of his father.

Trace always laced the stories with humor and told them with a lopsided grin, but she'd sensed the pain underneath. Nic had been touched that she'd seen that small layer of vulnerability from a man who operated at the highest levels of a government organization. Like it was only for her to see. Because it wasn't something he showed anyone else.

Ever.

She'd seen him debrief some of the worst specimens of human depravity without a single expression crossing his face.

Yet in those quiet moments together, she'd seen beneath the granite.

Saving Olivia Brigante and getting her to safety isn't about you and Trace.

Those internal admonitions reared up again, cutting through the morass of memory that threatened to pull her under.

She had to remember that. Had to keep it in the forefront of her thoughts. Old feelings and memories could not cloud this case or her judgment. The risks if she lost focus were simply too great.

"You think I need to look at the mother again?" she finally asked, surfacing from her thoughts.

Oblivious to her roiling emotions, Trace's response was as unyielding as his cold gray gaze. "Damn straight you do."

"Then on that we're agreed."

That gray heated slightly, and she took some small satisfaction that she'd tripped his expectations once again.

"That's what I've been doing for the last hour in my room. Digging into every single thing I know about the Brigante family and what we think."

"I thought you said Richie's business was the focus."

"It was. Until I asked the team to expand it and look at everyone in his orbit. His big sister and ex-wife were the top of the list since the Brigantes' parents are gone. There aren't any other close family members to consider."

"How deeply have you looked at the sister? The first time," he clarified.

"She was the first family member we evaluated after we put eyes on Richie. The ex-wife was duly reviewed, but early indications suggested she just wanted out of the marriage and that ultimately matched our discovery on her."

"Tell me what you know."

"Eloisa comes off like a caricature of a person. Part '40s movie star, part sly fox, part femme fatale. There's an affectation to her personality that's impossible to ignore. But—"

"But what?"

"I thinks she loves her family. And I do think she loves her child, but my assessment is she doesn't fully understand just how deep Olivia's intelligence goes."

"Surely Olivia's been tested through the years. Would a mother who cares about her child somehow miss that?"

It was a good question, and one Nic admittedly hadn't asked herself. Was she so determined to believe Olivia existed in a cocoon of protection that she'd misjudged Eloisa's intentions?

One more sign of how mixed up she was by this case.

"It's a fair point."

"Mothers know their children," Trace insisted.

Some don't.

The thought hung there, hovering between them, and she would have bet her very last penny Trace was thinking the same. But neither put voice to it, and before she could even think to find a way to manage that emotional minefield, he'd already moved on.

"So we go on the assumption Eloisa has a better handle on Olivia's skills than might appear." A thoughtful look carved Trace's features into deeply grooved lines. "And it would be the mother who had to let her go with the uncle if she's missing."

"He could have taken her."

"But nothing's pinged on the mother, right? No upset? No frantic calls."

"She's on a romantic trip with her new boyfriend."

"And isn't talking to the kid?"

They stared at each other, their next step immediately obvious, but Trace got to it first. "We need to put a tap on the mother."

"I can't just do that, Trace. I have to follow procedure, and a warrant's at the top of the list."

His answer was swift.

Immediate.

And exactly what she wanted to do.

"I don't."

Chapter 7

He had to tread carefully. It was the mental warning that had cautioned him since looking up to find Nic staring at him across the expanse of woods during his morning ride with Magnum. It had grown increasingly louder—like a drumbeat—as the day progressed.

It practically had his pulse thrumming out of his skin now.

But it was how he managed this current conversation that would really set the tone.

Trace eyed Nic, curious to see the quick expressions that flitted across her face—frustration to wry humor to what looked like acceptance. Nic seemed to experience them all as she considered his words.

"You with me on this?" he asked. "Or do you want me to go it alone?"

One last expression settled over her features at his question, a whip-quick flashover to anger. "I didn't come here to put this all on you."

"I'm not suggesting that. But you *are* still a federal employee. I've got a bit more latitude than you do."

"I came to you *because* you've got latitude," she said, winging his emphasis right back to him. "That doesn't change my responsibilities here."

"Okay then, we're agreed."

Nic looked about to argue, her mouth even opening before she snapped it shut as Trace continued.

"We put an illegal tap on the mother and see what we get."

"She's traveling with the boyfriend. She could be anywhere. Putting a tap on her home's not going to give us what we need."

"We'll go in through the phone. I can drop a piece of code via a text link, and we can get access to her calls and texts."

"You think she's just going to click it? From a strange text?"

"She will if we make it look good enough."

Trace was honest enough with himself that he could admit he was enjoying this more than a little bit. Nic might be determined to hold on to her bravado and do this the way he suggested, but she wasn't exactly comfortable, either.

It took him back to their earliest days together.

They'd disagreed about their work from the start. It had been fascinating at the beginning, getting her thoughts and opinions on the work and coming to understand how ironclad her principles were.

Had he ever had those?

Oh, he had his own code of honor, to be sure. But rigid, inflexible principles when it came to the work? Not so much.

He'd had a lot of successful cases because of it, too. Tossing the rule book out when his instincts grew too loud and resonant to ignore had not only served him well but had proven itself a sound strategy many times over.

Times that, Trace knew, he wouldn't have closed the work *without* breaking the rules.

But not Nic. She *was* the rule book.

Which made her willingness to go outside of it for this case all the evidence he needed to know that this mattered to her.

"How are you going to fool Eloisa?" Nic asked, obviously resigned to their next steps.

"We'll gin up a fake text based off of what she loves most. You said she's a fan of the fancy boyfriend. We can make a text from a high-end boutique or a high-end hotel for starters."

"She's not going to fall for it."

"It's my job to see that she does."

"Our job."

Although his memories of their time together had haunted him since Nic's arrival, something about the firm set of her jaw and the slightly mulish expression that thinned her mouth into a straight line pulled him up short. Like a rogue wave, the memory washed over him, so intense he wondered if his knees would have actually buckled had he been standing.

"What?" she asked, keying into his sudden mood change.

"Nothing."

"No, that look meant something."

"It's really nothing."

"Let me be the judge of that."

"I just—" He broke off, not sure why he suddenly felt so out of his depth when he'd distinctly felt the upper hand less than two minutes ago.

And yet…wasn't that the very definition of him and Nic?

"There was something about that expression on your face. It took me back for a moment."

She didn't speak and instead simply sat there with that intense gaze as she considered him. He was close to responding when she leaned forward a bit, her expression earnest.

"This whole day has been an experience in being taken back. Far more than I ever expected."

Whether it was the absolute honesty or just the fact that it was *her*—his Nic—back in his presence, Trace didn't know. "It's not how I expected my day to turn out, I'll give you that," he said. "But I am glad you're here. More than I'd have imagined I could be."

She extended her hand across the desk, laying it over his. "Even when I told myself it was a bad idea, I knew you were the answer, Trace."

He stared down at where their bodies joined, the heat of her palm searing the back of his hand.

They'd been the answer for one another for a long time, until one day, they weren't. It was that moment—the final one when he'd decided it was time to go away—that lingered now.

He hoped like hell he could be the man she needed this time.

Moments—heavy ones. Light ones. Soul-searing ones—had she really banked on all of this?

Nic asked herself that question as she slipped from Trace's office to go gather a few of her notes on Eloisa.

Her hand still tingled with heat where she'd laid it over his, and she fought off the urge to wiggle her fingers as if she could simply shake off the heat and need and sheer history that arced between them.

It was a quick trip to grab her file, but she used the time to try to regain her equilibrium.

Ignore the moments.

Keep your attention on the now.

Focus on what you came here to do.

It was a good idea until she was confronted by an impressive wall of men waiting for her in the kitchen.

"I pulled in reinforcements." Trace's comment was casual, but she sensed his intentions straight off.

Let them in, too.

It flew in the face of who she was—letting others in—but really, hadn't this entire case tested who she thought she was? More, who she *believed* she was.

"Sure. Great."

Garner and Jake—now fully clothed—both leaned back against various points on the kitchen counter. Hogan settled down, his head between his paws, beside Jake.

"Trace gave us rather limited details on what's going on," Garner started. "Why don't you walk us through it?"

Nic hadn't expected to pull additional people into this project, but as she took in the other two men, she realized it wasn't an entirely bad idea to get some fresh eyes on the case. Yes, Trace was fresh as of a few hours ago, but he was also former CIA. He was trained to look at data the same way she was.

Would Garner and Jake see something different?

She further consoled herself with one other key point. Whatever new life Trace had created for himself, it unquestionably included his brother. Now it included Jake, too, even if she did get the sense Trace was still trying to get his footing with the man. Something she'd keep an eye on and ask about later.

With a nod, she gestured toward the kitchen table and launched into a quick debrief on the case, including the steps taken up to now and what had brought her to Wyoming.

"You think the child's been taken?" Jake was the first to speak.

Nic considered how to answer. While moving a child to a place where she could be used for nefarious purposes was absolutely kidnapping, up until recently Olivia likely hadn't seen it that way. But this morning…

Nic. It's me Olivia. I'm in trouble.

The breach of Nic's systems this morning now suggested otherwise.

"I think she's being maneuvered, her skills used as a point of manipulation. Her outreach to me this morning suggests she's aware of this, which now risks our working assumption that she won't be hurt by her uncle."

"So let's make a plan and get her out." Garner's eyes lit with a simmering excitement she could feel arcing around the table.

"I'd like to, but actually finding her is the challenge."

Garner seemed undeterred by her pushback. "One we can surely get around. If she's with the uncle, we'll do some digging into his whereabouts."

"We can't run the risk of tipping him off, and I have no idea if he's got someone in the agency watching out for him." It pained Nic to even think something like that about her colleagues, but nothing was off the table. Especially since her senses had been on high alert that something was off about this job from the start.

A child was in danger, which was obviously her first priority. But their inability to dig into Brigante's financials with any level of success felt like a blocker that shouldn't have been quite so insurmountable.

Garner barely held back a snort. "Multilayered, inefficient bureaucracy at its finest."

Trace elbowed his brother. "You want to cool it?"

"Because ignoring the reality of the situation is somehow better?"

Nic's initial impression of Garner was a mix of loyal hard-ass and lighthearted jokester, but looking at him across the table—even with Trace trying to quiet him— she saw something more.

A man who carried so much resentment it had become a simmering rage below the surface.

What had happened to him?

Trace had never said much to her in the time they were together, beyond the cursory explanation that he had a brother who was a navy SEAL.

But here? Now? She saw a man as damaged as she suspected Trace was. Would that make the two of them stronger? Or would it send them down a rogue path, only exacerbated by their new addition, Jake?

As if sensing a need to break the tension, their third musketeer jumped in. "So what do we do?"

"I'm going to put a trace on the kid's mother's phone. She may be out getting her rocks off with her rich boyfriend, but she's bound to talk to the kid from time to time." Trace shrugged. "Or at least text."

"You doing the full rock star?" Garner asked, and Nic could only puzzle at the question.

"Rock star plus pampered princess."

"Oooh." Garner nodded. "Good one."

"Care to clue us in?" Jake finally asked, his head swiveling between the brothers.

Trace tapped the back of his cell phone, face down on the table in front of him. "We're going to make her think she's got street cred equivalent to a mix of Taylor Swift and Princess Kate."

"How you going to do that?" Jake asked.

"We'll fake an invitation via text. I was looking at her social media, and she's got a fascination with a very specific high-end boutique in New York. I'll start there with an offer of a personal appointment and see if she bites."

"On a random text from someone she doesn't know?" Jake shook his head. "The temptation to bet you the next round of drinks in town is strong, but somehow I'm afraid you're gonna be right on this."

Subtle amusement at their byplay morphed into a full-on laugh at the three of them.

"Next round of drinks is on me if Trace can make this work."

Three pairs of eyes lit up at Nic's offer, but it was the subtle glee that filled Trace's that confirmed just how determined he was to win.

"You're on, Miles."

Trace built out the details of his phishing text for Eloisa Brigante, then shifted focus toward creating the small piece of malware he was going to use to monitor activity on her phone.

"You need help on that?" Nic asked.

She had flitted around the kitchen, pulling together something for a late lunch, as he worked on his laptop. Garner and Jake had headed out for the stables, Hogan following along in their wake.

Jake had mentioned something about getting the lay of the land, and while Trace didn't doubt it was true—the former cop was now going to be a horse trainer at least some of the time—he also figured it was an excuse to give him and Nic some privacy.

With the scent of soup now wafting from the stove—what did they have in the house to make soup?—she rejoined him at the table.

"I think I've got it. It's a pretty simple piece of code. I just need to mask the number to make it look legit if she calls it. We'll know pretty quickly if she bites or not."

Nic shook her head. "Don't people know better than to click on strange links?"

"They do until that link might lead them to something they want."

She shot him a questioning eye but didn't respond. They'd both been on enough jobs to know that people who should know better often didn't *actually* know better when something enticing tugged at them.

Since that thought sat a bit too uncomfortably close to how the two of them had gotten together, Trace didn't say anything further, just focused on finishing the job.

"Am I being unrealistic to think that this is going to get us to her?"

Nic's question hung between them as Trace considered how to play this. She wanted reassurance, and he wasn't in a position to give that to her any longer. He didn't have government resources behind him, nor did he have access to some of the tools he used to have to get the job done. Sure, he was confident in his own skills, but it was a hell of a lot easier with the government's slick and shiny toys backing you up.

Did he believe they'd find Olivia? Yes, absolutely.

Did he think it would be easy? Hell no.

But he didn't say any of those things. Instead, he looked

at her over the edge of his laptop and purposely kept his expression blank. "It's a start."

"Right. Sure. Of course it is."

"I know it's hard when you're not accessing the snazzy tech we all got used to, but none of it replaces our training."

There had been a restlessness about her he'd observed since she arrived. It had ebbed and flowed, but since they'd made the decision to hack Eloisa's phone, it had ratcheted back up.

So it was a surprise to see her relatively still, that energy that had hummed around her leveling down.

"I keep falling back on the training, too. And then I second-guess myself that it won't be enough."

He understood that. Had discussed it at length with Garner when they made the decision to change their lives.

Yes, the move to Wyoming had a variety of facets, one of which was their desire to still help others. But they'd also realized that their training and skills were augmented with significant resources they could no longer access. So they'd agreed in advance they would take on the jobs they believed they had the skills to handle. Because while they both fully acknowledged their training was exceptional, neither of them were superhuman.

Extending the invite to Jake had included more of the same, ensuring his expectations were matched to what Trace and Garner had chosen to build in Liar's Gulch.

"It will be."

With the short malware program he'd written humming through its setup, Trace stood to get more coffee. He'd pretty well gotten rid of his hangover, but the lingering malaise from an evening full of far too many drinks—

coupled with the intense emotions at seeing Nic again—needed some sort of battle armor.

Caffeine would have to do.

The more enticing options that refused to leave his mind, all of which involved both of them shedding their clothes, weren't on the table. That particularly tantalizing outcome sat firmly in the realm of never-ever-again. He knew that.

And he'd known it the moment he walked out of her apartment all those long, lonely months ago.

The fact she'd shown up here—hunted him down, really—seeking his help wasn't going to change it.

Trace was surprised to see the slight shake of his hand as he poured the coffee into his mug, willing away that small sign of weakness. They were well-trained professionals. Considered spies in some quarters, excellent government assets in others.

They weren't lovers.

Not any longer.

Wishing he could change that flew in the face of every bit of rigorous discipline with which he lived his life.

He took a sip of the coffee, the ping from his computer drawing his attention. Satisfied he had his armor firmly back in place, he took his seat once more and reviewed the malware program he'd compiled for this job.

Coding wasn't his favorite portion of the work, but he'd gotten proficient enough through the years to know he'd done the basic job needed to track Olivia's mother and her communications. More important, he did it outside of Nic's work, so the ownership remained his. Although, was it splitting hairs since she *was* involved? If they found out, the government would most certainly see it that way.

Since his skills extended to destroying the evidence when they were done, he'd gamble on that split anyway.

Satisfied they had a path forward, he turned his laptop around on the kitchen table. "I think we're ready. Take a look at the text I've pulled together and let me know."

Nic's curious gaze had remained on him throughout their limited exchange, but she leaned forward and scanned his screen, her gaze narrowed slightly as she took in the words. "This is good. Smart to lean into the offer of a private shopping hour at her convenience."

"It's low-risk. And if we get in and see she has any issues with the boutique, we can smooth it over with a separate call." He grinned at her, wiggling his eyebrows. "I can play an indulgent rich boyfriend, ensuring my lady gets whatever she wants."

"This is really good, Trace. It's quick, efficient and easy to manage on our side." There wasn't any hint of censure or dismissal in her tone, so it made no sense that her comment pissed him off.

No sense at all.

Even if it did feel like a small pat on the head that he was a good boy.

But there was no mistaking the tightening of his chest or the way his response came out harsher than he intended. "That's why I'm here."

"Well, yeah. I mean—" She stopped, seeming to catch herself. "Are you upset about something?"

"No."

"Trace—"

"I'm not upset. I'm being an ass, and it's all on me."

"Why?"

Once again, there wasn't a hint of censure in her voice. There was the obvious question in her eyes as to what his problem was, but how did he explain that even he couldn't explain it?

"Can I send the text?"

"Of course." Nic lightly pushed the laptop back to him before standing and crossing to the stove to check the soup.

He wanted to apologize—knew he needed to—but for what? Feeling grumpy that she was only here because he was some sort of professional tool that she needed?

It was tempting to marinate in that place, but he had a job to do and time was wasting. With a tap on the keyboard, he hit Send on the fake text.

"Done."

"Thank you." Nic turned after she laid down the spoon she'd used to stir the pot. "And now I think we need to talk."

"Haven't we been doing that?"

"A bit. But we've also been letting old animosities mess up a lot of the words in between snatches of conversation, and it has to stop. I trust you, Trace. Implicitly, or I wouldn't be here."

Of course she was right. And he could sit and marinate even further in resentment that she'd been mature enough to admit it first, or he could own his part in it all.

His vacillating emotions had no place in this.

"I don't want to fight with you," he said on a small sigh. "And I'm glad you're here. Even happier that you felt you could come to me with this."

"Why do I hear a but?"

She might have taken ownership of her emotions first, but he wasn't that far behind. Whatever else they'd shared before it all imploded, they'd always been honest with each other.

Or he had been, save one small point. He loved her. To distraction.

And he'd never said a word.

That was his problem, and he'd spent the past two years working on putting it all behind him. Her coming to him for help couldn't change that. But it did mean there was history they needed to acknowledge. Maybe putting it out there would finally excise it from memory.

"Because we had a relationship. It doesn't matter how it ended, it doesn't erase that we had one. That's the 'but' between us, Nic. It's not going to go away."

"I know."

"So what do we do about it?"

"We put the mission first. Like always."

The words were straight up Nicola Miles. Sharp. Deliberate. To the point.

Even if the small hitch when she said *always* was as audible as a gunshot.

"Of course we do." He nodded as he stood from his seat and slowly crossed the kitchen toward her.

He knew she was right. He even agreed with her. But something had settled deep inside of him at that subtle hitch in her voice. That small, ever-so-slight clue that she wasn't as unaffected as she claimed, no matter what.

Like catching a tiger by the tail, he had no idea what he'd do once he proved his point, but he seemed determined to try anyway.

So he moved forward, narrowing the distance between them.

And leaped to cover her, dragging her to the kitchen floor, when the distinct sound of gunfire erupted just beyond the window.

Chapter 8

"Let me up!" Nic struggled under Trace's heavy weight—how did such a lanky man have such muscle mass?—desperate to get outside. Who was shooting at them? And what horror had she brought to his home? "Trace! Let. Me. Up."

He rolled to the side, still holding tight to her forearm when she lifted out of a crouch to look out the window.

"You don't know what's out there," he hissed.

"Which is why." She gritted her answer through her teeth as she tamped down on the immediate instinct to break his hold—and possibly his arm. "I'm a federal agent trained to go handle it."

Something shifted in his demeanor, and she sensed she'd finally gotten through to him when his grip loosened, but he still held her down by his side. "We can stay below the window line if we go behind the table."

"Let's go then."

She didn't wait for a response and instead dropped to her belly, army crawling past the exterior wall. Who had found her? It was the only question racing through her mind as she crawled through the kitchen.

The distinct ring of a cell phone pealed, and she heard

Trace answer gruffly before he shouted to her. "Wait, Nic! It's Garner."

With the wall still at her back, Nic leaned against it, her gaze on Trace's face as he switched to speaker.

"What have you got?"

"Jake and I are in the stables. Bastard's roaming around outside and thought he could get a shot off at us."

"That's a pretty bad way to announce your presence," Nic murmured.

"Exactly!" Garner's words came winging through the speaker. "It's a message, and I'm not quite sure what he's hoping to convey. Especially since we can't find a second, either, and we've both been on the cameras in the office."

Nic didn't recall seeing a video array in the stables but didn't doubt they had one.

"You have eyes on him?" Trace asked.

"I did until he moved out of sight toward the house. That dead space you and I keep meaning to fix. Jake and I will cover you from out here. Keep me on the line so I can watch your back and watch yourselves."

"We've got it. I'm leaving the line open and putting my earbuds in."

"You on dual use?" Garner asked.

"Of course." Trace tucked the phone back in his pocket, Garner's voice evaporating with the switch to his earbuds.

Nic extended a hand. "Give me one."

He nodded, pulling out an earbud and handing it to her before pointing toward the sliding back door. "Let's bypass the living room and head for the laundry room."

"Or we can split up and have a better chance of finding him."

"It's a risk. You're not armed."

She grinned before tapping her calf. "Oh, sweet summer child, guess again."

Where the old Trace might have taken offense at the sarcasm, this version simply grinned and nodded. "Of course."

"But you're not."

"Shall I make you eat your words?" Trace reached behind his back and pulled out a handgun. "I snagged a bit of backup after the kid hacked into your system."

"Then we avoid the living room. You take the utility room, and I'll take the front door. Let's figure out what we're dealing with." Nic didn't wait for his agreement but headed for the front door, bypassing the living room and the wide sliding door that overlooked the back of the house.

Garner's assessment rang in her head as she moved rapidly through the space. *It's a message, and I'm not quite sure what he's hoping to convey.*

Who knew she was here? And so soon? She'd been careful, damn it. Was it someone from the agency, trying to thwart her attempts to find Olivia? If it was, she had a much bigger problem than she could have imagined.

Or did Richie Brigante actually act this quickly? If he did, that meant he and his goons were a lot closer than she initially estimated.

Nic sighed as she approached the oversize steel front door. First they had to catch the intruder, and then she could figure out where he'd come from.

She opened the door, careful to move it inch by inch so that she wasn't an immediate target. When the crack was wide enough, she took a chance to look outside, only to see the air continue to bluster in thick swirls, kicking up leaves and grass in its wake.

The direct line in her earbud carried a steady stream of instructions from Garner. She could even hear Jake giving updates on what he saw on the cameras. All of which confirmed the intruder had wisped away like smoke.

Slipping outside, she held still, trying to listen for some clue as to where their attacker had gone. Although Garner's comments were direct and issued only when necessary, it was still distracting to have the noise, and she listened with focused attention, trying to catch something—a snapped branch or a scuffed foot on the driveway or *anything*—on the air.

Only to still come up with nothing.

She'd nearly begun moving again when she caught the faintest glimmer of something. An instinct, really, that had her whirling toward the far side of the driveway.

Only to feel the distinct press of a gun at her temple, the air blustering around her in thick gusts.

Trace hated the waiting.

He'd always hated the waiting part of his job but had managed to forget just how much of it he used to do.

Waiting for orders.

Waiting for the time to take action.

Waiting for the object of his mission to make a move.

It had always held an endless quality that never fully faded, even after the adrenaline rush when things finally shifted into all-out action and fierce battle.

He wasn't sure what that said about him, but he knew himself well enough to know it was his own personal truth.

It wasn't a lack of patience, either. He had plenty of it—and had proven it to himself over and over in his work with the horses.

But he had zero tolerance anymore for the endless waiting that came on an op.

Which made the small, calm voice that echoed in his ear both a shock and an instant cattle prod into motion.

"Trace. Do you remember Reykjavík?" The tone in her voice was as fragile as glass.

Already on the move, he cycled through the ops they'd shared during their time working together, before landing on the memory she wanted him to recall.

Iceland.

New Year's Eve.

And a shooter waiting just outside the door, somehow managing to get the two of them apart.

"Garner." He whipped out orders with deadly calm as he moved. "Get Jake and get out of the barn. He's got her at the front door. Approach right flank. I've got the left."

An expletive exploded in his ear, a match for the one cycling through his head.

How had they missed this?

But Garner's mention of their dead spaces was spot-on. They had one at the side of the house, too. A problem he'd been meaning to fix, but he'd tabled it knowing they had enough other cameras around the house that they'd know of an intruder long before one got to the front door.

How's that working out for ya, Withrow?

Vowing to go over it endlessly later, he stilled just shy of the front of the house. His head was already upside down because Nic was here. Barreling in without taking a moment was akin to putting a bullet in her head.

"I'm almost there." Garner's voice was a whisper in his ear, and Trace took some solace that Nic would have heard it too.

"I'm closer."

"Jake stayed in the office. He's got eyes on them, and guy's got her just outside the front door. I've got comms in my other ear. On my mark, Trace."

"Noted," Trace whispered, well aware Nic's captor might hear him but not caring any longer.

"Now!"

Trace moved in time with his brother's shout as the world went eerily still, even as his body was in full motion, operating on sheer instinct and adrenaline. He ran straight for Nic, Garner coming from the other direction.

As Trace rounded the corner, the vision of her held in the grip of the intruder nearly felled him, but he kept moving, focused on neutralizing the situation.

He couldn't think about the fact that it was *her.*

He had to focus on the threat.

Focus, damn it.

His head swirled at the risks to her, but he kept moving. Kept straight for the man who held her in his grip, who now had the immediate threat of Garner heading for him as well.

But it was Nic's war cry that erupted into the air, her arm lifting and slamming into the guy's arm and chin, disrupting his equilibrium with the mix of motion and noise.

The three of them worked as a unit, Nic making the immediate hits to the intruder's body to disable him while Trace approached from the back and Garner ran point, removing the man's weapons from the front.

"Who are you?" Trace pulled hard on the man's arms, now behind his back.

"Amateurs." The man spat the word, followed by an actual well of spit in Nic's direction.

Trace tightened his hold, but it was his brother who moved right into the potential line of unsanitary fire.

Garner's gaze was hard, but his smile was pure menace and mischief all rolled into one as he leaned in close to the man's face. "Since we're the ones standing here and you're trussed up like a turkey ready for dinner, I'd guess again."

"Spare me. You didn't know I was here until I wanted you to know."

Although it was true, Trace held still, not wanting any response to seem like weakness or worse, agreement.

"Again, I repeat my point," Garner said. "You're the one standing here trussed up between the three of us."

Even though he couldn't see the intruder's face, Trace easily pictured the sneer that settled there. "You have no idea what she's dragged to your door."

"Then enlighten us." Nic's voice was steady and deadly calm.

"You think this is about a kid."

Nic's stare was unrelenting as she gazed at the man Trace held still. "I think there's a child being used as a pawn, but I don't think any of this is about a kid."

"They're never going to let you have her."

The flash in that crystal-blue gaze was brief, but Trace saw it all the same.

They.

It was small, but it was a slip.

"She's not a bargaining chip," Nic insisted.

"Then I guess you're out of aces," the man said.

Their quarry had remained eerily still through the exchange, not displaying any signs of struggle as he remained inside of Trace's hold. All that vanished when he moved suddenly, obviously determined to do some sort of damage.

Trace held tight and nearly had him in place, Garner

moving up to add his additional weight, when the guy got free of both of them. Where the man thought he'd go with three people immediately on his tail, Trace didn't know, but he keenly understood the need for escape.

Trace, Nic and Garner took off in pursuit, racing down the front path of the house following the intruder.

Only to come to a slamming halt as the man's body shook violently, felled in the face of an unstoppable force.

Nic felt the rush of air before she even registered the bullet. She ran past the intruder, as did Trace and Garner, until they all realized what happened and doubled back.

"Sniper!" Trace called it first as they all quickly dropped to the ground. "Get to the tree line!"

Employing the same belly crawl she'd used in the ranch kitchen, Nic moved away from the body, seeking cover in the foliage that surrounded the property.

Foliage that had hidden a sniper and who-knew-what level of backup for the guy who'd made a run at them.

"Who is he?" Trace asked as he assessed their surroundings.

"No idea." Nic shook her head. "He's not familiar nor have I seen him in the Brigante files."

"Highly paid mercenary, most likely," Garner added before shifting back to work with Jake on their linked comms.

"Who's tracking you, and how the hell did they find you here?" Trace glanced at the body, his features taut from the stress of the moment. "And if you keep holding out on me, you can get off my property now."

"I'm not holding out on you. I've told you everything."

"Including whatever BS you've been facing in the

home office?" Anger filled his lean features, driving deep, craggy lines into his forehead and around his eyes.

She knew that look—had seen it more than once—but never had she seen the absolute exhaustion behind it. Nor had she seen the very thin threads he was hanging on to as he worked to keep it together.

"I have told you what I know. Everything I know. But you have to know I came to you because I wasn't comfortable in the home office." She kept her gaze on his, willing him to understand.

"You haven't told me who. Who do you suspect, Nic?"

"I would never have taken this option if I thought there was any other way back in DC."

"Not what I asked you." He shook his head. "I asked you who."

"I can't tell you that."

"You come to my home. You hold a gun on me. You drag me into this. And I don't have a right to know?"

"I can't tell you that because I don't know."

"Well, hell."

Well, hell was right. But Nic didn't know how to fix it or how to give him a different answer. She did think the problems were buried somewhere deep inside the agency, even if she couldn't prove it.

But it was that belief that had spurred her on to find Trace.

She'd never have come to him if she'd had a choice. But she couldn't work inside the office, either. And she couldn't do this alone. Whatever else she'd figured out these past months, it was that.

So she'd gone to the one person she believed would handle this as faithfully as she would.

And the broken heart of the woman who'd loved him once upon a time would simply have to bear it.

"We need to go deal with the body."

She was already on her feet and moving to do just that when Trace spoke. "We don't know the scene is clear."

"I'll take my chances."

It was risky, but her gut told her if a sniper was waiting to shoot them they'd have not only done it sooner, but they wouldn't have wasted time with the goon they sent in as advance reconnaissance.

Which only added to the mystery of it all.

Was the goon a mercenary sent in by the Brigante organization? Or was it someone back in DC trying to send her a message?

I asked you who.

Trace's words still echoed between them, a lingering admonishment that she wasn't doing anything to build trust with the one person she couldn't afford to piss off. But since she'd obviously passed that milestone more than a few times since arriving, she'd have to push it aside.

Kneeling down beside the body, she felt around his thick coat looking for any form of ID she already knew she wouldn't find.

She searched anyway because action was better than inertia. Trying to find answers was better than accepting that someone was trying to hide them.

And immersing herself in work was the only possible protection she had to get through this, find Olivia and get out of Wyoming.

"Are you sure you trust her?" Garner asked as he dragged a tarp, laden with the body, between him and Trace.

"I do."

"Is this ancient history talking?"

Trace considered his brother's question—well aware *ancient history* increasingly felt like the present—as he came to a halt at the stable doors.

"I actually do, in spite of our ancient—" He broke off, done with the euphemism. "In spite of our past relationship."

"So you're staying in this?" Garner pressed.

"I am." Trace pulled open the heavy stable doors. "That doesn't mean you and Jake have to."

"Ride or die, brother." Garner sighed as he bent to grab handfuls of tarp again. "I'm yours."

"I know." Trace stilled and stared at his brother. "And I also know what that support means."

"Don't get mushy."

Despite the intense day—and the dead body between them—Garner's grin was broad and full of humor, and Trace couldn't help but smile back.

"You're an ass."

"Of the first water."

Trace shook his head before adding his muscle to move the body. They ultimately settled the dead man in an empty stall. He'd call local law enforcement and explain the situation. The fact that they had cameras on the property would work in their favor, the videos showing clear proof they were attacked and defending themselves.

The issue was how quickly should he call them in.

The bad weather that had been reported all week looked imminent, the skies growing darker since morning. He wasn't interested in putting local law enforcement in danger if there were others lurking around the property.

Garner stepped around the body and headed for the

long pathway that ran down the length of the barn. "Let's go see if Jake's found anything else."

"I was coming to find you." Jake met them halfway down the stable aisle, several horses poking their heads over their stall doors at the man's obvious excitement.

"Someone else out there?" Trace was already on the move, heading for the office and the high-tech security setup they housed there.

"I haven't found anyone else. I've rewound the tapes by twenty-four hours but will keep looking. But I did find our dude lurking around this morning, just after ten, on what looks to be the very edge of the property."

Trace did the quick math and realized he'd already run into Nic in the woods and brought her back to the house by then. Had it really only been that morning? "Can you cue it up for me?"

"Already there." In the office, Jake tapped a few keys, obviously well-versed in visual technology tools the way he seamlessly shifted between screens and various commands to view the footage.

Trace focused on the top screen where the video was cued up, Garner leaning in with him. They took in the intruder's familiar figure, lurking around the edge of the property. The guy moved with purpose, but he didn't communicate via any device, nor did he refer to any digital technology.

"It's a match." Trace knocked his knuckles on the narrow table that ran the length of the viewing console. "He's not using any tech, and we didn't find anything on him."

"You'd give up your tech?" Garner glanced toward Trace.

Jake let out a low whistle and added a quiet "hell no."

"Not if given an option." Trace considered some of the more difficult missions he'd run. Tech was dangerous because if it got into the wrong hands, the ramifications on discovery were huge. But to be without anything?

"So who took away his option?" Garner reached over and tapped a few keys, rewinding the video before pausing it on a specific frame. "There. See how he's looking backward?"

Trace had seen the same and intended to look once more when they ran through it again. "How much you want to bet the sniper is who he was looking at? Maybe he was still communicating with him in some way."

"I don't take sucker bets," Garner said. "And that would be the very definition of one. He's working with someone, and once he wasn't useful anymore, that someone shot him."

They watched the recording a few more times before shifting to the other items Jake had cued up.

"You've got a few dead spots, but I was able to piece his movements together, going out of frame on one camera and back in on another."

"That was a deliberate decision. We can't reasonably cover the entire property, so we picked key spots."

"Except around the house," Trace corrected his brother. "We need to fix that."

"Yeah, we do."

Garner's agreement was obvious, but it still stuck an incredibly hard landing in Trace's gut that Nic had been attacked the way she had. If the mercenary—and Trace was working off the assumption the guy *was* hired muscle—hadn't gone after Garner and Jake first, who knew what could have happened?

"We need to find the sniper. We've got general direction, and there may be something up there we can use."

"You really think so?"

Trace turned at Nic's voice, eyeing her where she stood in the doorway to the office.

"I think that's the next step. The guy didn't get on the property by accident, and he sure as hell wasn't murdered because he stumbled into the wrong place."

"I'll get the body dealt with," Nic said, "and then I'm going to get backup. They'll either send a field team to me, or we'll work the project from DC. Either way, you don't need me bringing this sort of violence to your door."

"You think we're afraid of a few bullets?" Jake asked.

It was unexpected to hear their newcomer pipe up so quickly, and all heads turned toward the former Vegas cop with a past full of baggage. Or at least that was what Trace assumed, and Jake hadn't given him any reason to think otherwise.

"I think we should all be afraid," Nic said. "What just happened out there was a major escalation."

Obviously undeterred, Jake persisted, "It was also a really bad tip of the hand." When no one said anything, he laid out his argument. "If it's Brigante's people, they tipped their hand. And if it's your old office mates…" Jake tilted his head toward Trace "…it's extra bad form."

Although he couldn't fault the logic, Trace was fascinated by how quickly Jake pulled the pieces together without the benefit of time or experience with the federal government. "Some of the boys and girls at the agency were never taught to play nice." He couldn't resist adding, "I know because I was one of them."

"You played by the rules."

Nic's ready defense captured him, and he couldn't resist poking that old topic just a bit. "We both know only when it suited me. It was the biggest reason we broke up."

"No it wasn't."

Trace suddenly recognized his tactical error as his brother and his new roommate both became very interested in whatever was coming next.

He'd put their personal life on display and based on the light of battle filling her vivid blue gaze, Nic wasn't going to wait to argue with him outside the surveillance of two deeply interested parties.

"We broke up because you didn't trust me to have your back."

"I always trusted you."

"No, Trace, you didn't. Not when it mattered most."

Chapter 9

Nic cursed herself a million ways to Sunday that she'd let something that personal slip out. In front of others, no less. One more sign the feelings she carried for him—the ones she never actually dealt with, just buried deep—carried the very real risk of overshadowing what she was here to do.

And she could not let that happen.

Olivia was the focus.

All the rest—catching Brigante, dealing with possible rot back in DC, even those overwhelming feelings—they all had to come second.

A child's life was at stake.

She had to keep that focus, or else…

The thought faded away, replaced with the truth.

For all her armor and all her belief that she could have a physical affair with Trace Withrow and move on, it had been the biggest lie she'd ever told herself. The relationship had had the most impactful one of her life, and she hadn't survived the end of it quite the way she'd believed she could when it all began.

But that was her secret.

Her burden.

She'd remained strong for two years, moving on in life if not in spirit. And she had to keep doing it.

Because right now, Olivia's life was all that mattered.

"Much as I'd like to stand here and continue this little coffee klatch slash jaunt down memory lane, we need to find where the sniper set up. I doubt we'll find any clues, but we have to try." She turned on a heel and headed for the exit to the stables, not surprised when she heard footsteps behind her, stopping her before she hit the door.

"Nic. Wait."

"We don't have time to wait."

"Nic!"

She felt the light tug on her hand, and she turned to face Trace, pulling her hand free of his grip. "Can we at least talk on the move?"

"Fine. We keep extra tools here in the stables. Let's suit up in Kevlar and take the truck. I have an idea of where the sniper set up to get that sort of view on the front of the house."

Since going out unarmed with a sharpshooter on the loose was the height of stupidity, she nodded and followed him to a long wall of closets. She'd assumed they all held tack and other items for the horses when she passed them earlier, but when Trace opened the last cabinet in the row, she saw what he'd promised.

State-of-the-art physical protection.

"How much did you and Garner put into this place?"

"Enough," he muttered as he pulled out a jacket for her, followed by one for himself.

The thick body armor was tight when she zipped it up—well fitted as it should be—and she felt an odd calming inside at the additional layer of protection.

It was a counterpoint to just how vulnerable she'd felt outside with the guy who'd attacked them. While the body armor wouldn't protect her from a head shot, it went a long way toward making her feel better if they got into a skirmish.

"Let's go," Trace said and she didn't miss the light of battle that filled his gray eyes.

She headed for the work truck parked outside the stables and climbed into the passenger seat. Trace climbed into the driver seat and in moments had them turned around and heading down the long driveway that led to the ranch house.

"What are you going to do with the body?"

"We have a good relationship with local law enforcement. Working with them isn't the problem." Trace glanced over at her as he took a right onto a dirt road that would take them into the heart of the ranch. "The question is when. I don't want them tipping off anyone at the agency that you're here."

"You don't have to hold off on my account."

"I think I do. And I think you're fooling yourself if you think otherwise."

Trace's words were calm and level, a counterpoint to the muscle that ticked in his jaw and the hard set of his face.

He was pissed off.

She recognized the surly attitude. Faced it before, as a matter of fact. Trace was a world champion blusterer when properly ruffled. It was actually a trait she'd admired. There was no hiding his emotions. No faking a smile when he was pissed off or giving someone hell for making mistakes on an op.

Or, as most often was the case, giving that hell to himself because he hadn't met his own exceptionally high standards.

So yes, she'd seen this side of him. But then they were

colleagues. Mission buddies. And later lovers. There was an intimacy to all that had come before that they no longer shared.

Memories of intimacy weren't the same as actual intimacy, and that suddenly seemed very important.

In the past, she'd known the right words or even a joke to ease the situation. Now she had nothing to defuse the tension. Which only left her to her silence and him to simmer beside her, a bubbling cauldron building steam.

They continued on the trail for a short while before he turned off, the land beneath the truck growing increasingly bumpy and rough. They didn't go much more than half a mile when he came to a halt, pulling the truck to the side.

"We'll walk the rest of the way."

Nic followed Trace through the thick brush, this portion of the land rugged and harsh and likely why the ranch house was set where it was. Although she hadn't seen the full property, the thick ridge that made up this portion likely made it difficult to manage with livestock or to use for farmland.

"Is this ridge the reason the house and stables are set where they are?"

"Yep. Workable areas were left open while this area below the ridge made it ideal to hold people and animals."

"It's clever," Nic observed as they walked, taking in the land and the rising height.

"It was one of the things that sold me on the place. That thoughtfulness about the layout and the use of the land. People on a ranch have to live somewhere, so put them in the place that's least useful to the business endeavors of the property."

"Hearty people conquered this land." She glanced sideways, curious to see the fresh air and walk hadn't done anything to change his mood or the dark look that rode his features. "Hearty people continue to make it home."

"Yes."

"Look, Trace." She stopped, trying to get him to slow down for a minute and snap out of this mood that he seemed determined to marinate in. "I get this is not ideal, and I've shown up in your life and created chaos with seeming ease. But talk to me. What has you so upset?"

"You mean besides the gun aimed at me to start my day, the very real knowledge a child is in danger, and then an assassin on my property who was determined to kill you and whomever else got in his way?"

"We're handling it."

"By slapping on Kevlar and hunting down a sniper? That's handling it?"

"Trace, I—"

The words died as he stopped and stared at her. Right there, in the midst of the dying afternoon light and the cold air that swirled around them and the very real knowledge that they had no idea who hunted them. "You what? You going to apologize again?"

"No, I think the time for that's past. I just…"

The words faded out again, an embarrassing state that she couldn't seem to shake. She didn't forget her words. Nor did she back down from the face of a fight.

But this? The sheer anger that rode his features?

"What has you so riled up? I get this is all an inconvenience, and I've dropped your old life smack in the middle of your new one. But we've got a plan. We'll get Olivia, and I'll be gone."

A harsh laugh escaped his lips, and she felt that tugging sensation that pulled her from way down deep inside. "Same old Nic. Blind devotion to the job and blithe ignorance to your own personal danger."

"What does that mean?" Just because she was willing to acknowledge his anger didn't mean she refused to allow her own to rise. Whatever had him in knots didn't mean she had to bear the brunt.

"Did you give any thought to the danger you've taken on, doing this by yourself? Outside the auspices of the agency?"

"I came to you."

"Now! But how long have you been in the thick of this? Alone!"

Whatever worry they'd both carried about being spotted by the sniper had faded. Lunacy? Yes, probably. But if they were really targets, they'd likely have been shot at already. "I came to you, Trace. You have to know what that cost me!"

"Yes, I know. I know exactly what it cost you because I'm paying the same damn price, with interest."

"What's that supposed to mean?"

"I watched him hold you. Press a gun to your forehead. That's the danger that's been stalking you. You, Nic!"

With startling clarity, the reason for his ire and frustration became clear. This wasn't about a shooter or a case or even her holding a gun on him this morning.

It was about *her*.

Before the knowledge had even fully sunk in, she felt herself being dragged forward. The thick Kevlar made a hard barrier between them when he pulled her close, but she didn't have time to worry about it as his mouth came over hers.

Crushing.

Devouring.

Feasting.

As she wrapped her arms around his waist, just below the thick band of protection, she matched his ardor.

And gave up the ridiculous notion that there was any possible way she could ever keep her heart out of this.

Trace kept a firm hold on her, the sheer wonder at having her in his arms again juxtaposed by the thick protective material between them and the reality that they were standing in the woods mere yards from where a sniper had hid less than an hour before.

Had he lost every bit of training and ability he'd honed over decades?

Even as something in the back of his mind recognized they were still in danger, something more present—and far more fierce—beat in his blood.

He needed this. Desperately.

Because one wrong move, and she'd have died today.

The man who attacked Nic had been determined to cause problems, and it was only by sheer luck Trace had gotten to her first. It was only the man's extreme bad fortune to get himself involved with some ruthless machine who only ever intended to use him as a pawn.

Trace knew he should pay attention to all of that. That he should dig down deep and let his exhaustive training and years of reading the worst of humanity's actions be his guide.

But all he wanted was Nic. And these quiet, nearly desperate moments to hold her close and make them both remember what had burned so bright and clear between them.

God, he'd missed her.

More, he'd missed *them*. What it felt like to be with

her and how he felt when he was with her. Free in a way he'd never experienced before or since.

With all that swirling in his mind, Trace pushed every one of those emotions into the kiss. It was hot and carnal and oddly sweet at the same time. Because whatever he'd remembered of her, nothing could compare to having her in his arms once more.

Danger be damned.

"Trace." His name was half moan, half sigh against his lips. "We can't do this here."

His response was wholly inappropriate, but he found he couldn't stop the smile as he pulled back slightly to look down at her. "We've already made easy targets of ourselves, and no bullets yet. I think we're safe."

Her eyebrows rose over those gorgeous blue eyes, and he saw skepticism rapidly chasing away desire. "That's a way to look at it."

"I'm not apologizing for taking a moment."

"I'm—" She took a deep breath. "I'm not apologizing, either. But we need to focus on the sniper."

"I'll bet you another kiss we're not going to find anything."

"Not taking that bet, and we're not kissing again."

Trace nearly laughed out loud at the prim response and decided to save any smart-ass remarks for later. Because after what they just shared, he was quite sure that wasn't their last kiss.

But he'd leave her to her illusions.

"Fine then, let's look."

He continued tramping up the dirt path that led to the upper portion of the ridge. While he wasn't convinced they'd find anything left behind, like shell casings or a lost glove, he was interested in what they could potentially track.

Footprints. The imprint of heavy equipment like a tripod to balance a rifle. Or even a body print if the sniper lay prone on the ground to take the shot.

Their recent weather was a positive in the tracking work—the late winter snows and the corresponding snowmelt after a few unexpectedly sunny days had made the ground soft. And no sniper, no matter how good, could erase the pull of gravity.

The path they walked was clear, so Trace shifted his attention to the scrub grass alongside the trail. His patience was rewarded when he got the distinct imprints for two pairs of shoes.

"Here." He waved Nic over. "Look here."

"So they were together."

"Yep. And that's cold. They come up here like partners in crime, but one knows the other's unlikely to leave."

Nic knelt down to inspect the footprints before looking back up at him. "You think he was expendable from the first?"

"If he'd succeeded, maybe not. Likely not, as the sniper would have needed to come play backup to deal with the rest of us." Trace looked around, curious now that he considered that angle. "Jake would have been a surprise since he just got here. Maybe they figured they could take us three to two. It's not a secret my brother lives here."

"And your ranch hands. They would have been targets, too. It seems risky to think anyone could have come onto this property and thought they could simply slaughter everyone." Nic stood, shaking her head. "And even that. I just got here this morning. How could anyone plan it so fast? Even if Brigante is that connected, Olivia just hacked into my computer a few hours ago. None of this makes sense."

Trace had to agree with her assessment. Nothing about the attacker and the shooter up on the ridge fit any logical pattern. "You thought someone back in the home office could be involved. They'd have time to get here and set this up."

"Trace, I know you don't fully believe me on that front, but I've been careful at the office. And that's with not even being quite sure anyone at the office is even the problem."

"But you've considered it?" he pressed.

"Of course. I won't rule it out until everyone can be fully ruled out. It's why I haven't shared my theories with anyone and covered my tracks on my trip out here."

"How'd you get here?"

"I scheduled a few personal days. I flew to Florida first and spent the weekend there. Then I went on to Denver. Then I rented a car to drive up here."

"You could have been tracked."

"Could have been, sure. But I was careful, I was on my guard every step of the way and never saw a tail, and I truly played up being out. I briefed everyone on my plans and had an action plan for covering my work while I was gone. Other than my computer log-ins, which I said I'd do to be available while remote, I've been careful."

Every point was fair and logical, and Trace wanted to believe she was right. But he also had a dead man on his property and a case suspicious enough that Nic was keeping it close to the vest *and* coming to him for help.

He wasn't ready to rule out his old employer as the root of the problem.

But, Trace admitted to himself on a sigh, he couldn't

let his old resentments lead the witness, either. "Let's keep going."

They followed the dual footprints until they came to the top of the ridge. Trace turned and could see the front door of the house clearly from where they stood. The ground was trampled in a circle around what was clearly three divots from a tripod. "Sniper was here."

He moved to stand in the line of sight again, but Nic beat him there, positioning herself as if she stood behind the sniper's rifle, looking through the sight down toward the house.

"Right here." Nic pulled out her phone and started snapping photos.

Trace busied himself with the footprints. They were large—he placed his own size twelves next to both sets and could see a fairly close match. "Looks like both snipers were male based on the prints. Since they didn't go back down the ridge side by side, I'm going to check the descent and see if anything's there."

He moved toward the other side of the trail, curious to see that there was one set of prints. He would investigate further but assumed he and Nic would be able to follow them back down. Likely this was the attacker leaving the vantage point to head down earlier and make trouble at the house.

But where were the other ones?

Retracing his steps, he moved back up to the vantage point and looked around, finally spotting the second set of prints down the back side of the ridge.

The escape.

It still bothered him that either man had gotten on the property undetected, but the exit was interesting. Since it was different from where the pair ascended the ridge,

Trace questioned if there was some sort of getaway car waiting on the other side.

"Nic, play something out with me." He waved her over, memories of their time in the field together filling his mind unexpectedly.

How seamlessly they worked together.

The way he'd bounce things off of her, spinning theories and watching as she was able to poke holes where needed or where she helped make the thread even stronger.

She came up beside him, oblivious to his wandering thoughts, her gaze on him telegraphing that she was firmly in huntress mode. "What are you thinking?"

"Two pairs of prints up the ridge. One down the back here. They didn't come in from this direction." Trace pointed to the back side and the lone set of footprints.

"You think there was a getaway car?"

"Yep. One our dead guy had no idea about."

"A driver and a third person involved?"

"A third doesn't make a lot of tactical sense. Why only send one down to deal with us if you had backup? You only need one sniper."

"True." She nodded, warming to the topic. "But that means if they came in together, they were in a different vehicle than the getaway car."

In unison, their gazes clashed, a triumphant note echoing from their words at the same time. "Let's find the car."

It was a good plan.

An excellent one, Trace knew.

They could come back later, but it was time to head out and find the car.

His focus was on the end game, so he'd chalk it up to his training that at the last minute he stopped and took one last look at the ridge, his gaze drifting over the ground.

That was when he saw it.

A glint of light, reflecting from where something metallic was buried in the grass.

He moved closer, curious, even as a wave of anticipation flew through him. Shell casing or maybe something that fell off a sniper's equipment?

That was his expectation when he bent down.

But as his fingers grazed the edge of a round disc, something dark and dangerous flashed in his mind as he picked up the small coin.

He knew what this was.

"Nic. Come here."

"What?" She moved closer immediately, obviously drawn by the urgency in his tone.

"Tell me you know what this is." He extended his hand, the coin lying flat in his palm.

"It's a challenge coin."

"It most certainly is. And last time I checked, these were most definitely a law enforcement thing. Not the work of shipping magnates."

Nic stared at the challenge coin displayed on Trace's palm and tried to catch her breath. She knew that coin.

Had one of her own, in fact.

"Those were given out when Roger Bane retired."

"Yeah, they were." Trace nodded, his gaze dark yet surprisingly unreadable. Even with the strangely damning evidence, it was the fact that she couldn't read him that ratcheted up her anxiety.

Roger had been their collective lead when they worked together. Incredibly well respected, he'd run his unit at the agency with a mix of humor, grace and integrity.

"Roger's been gone a little over two years."

"I know. His retirement was the reason I finally put in my resignation. I wasn't interested in staying in that place if Bane wasn't there, and Rannell wasn't sad to see me go. After all those years, he accepted my resignation and said it was probably 'for the best.'"

Unbidden, one of their last conversations before their relationship exploded ran through her mind.

There's an undercurrent here, Nic. Can't you feel it? Don't you sense it?

We work for a highly respected government agency.

With huge pockets of work subject to no external oversight.

We're keeping state secrets. What do you expect?

She'd argued those points at that time. They had latitude because of what they did. And the reality that in order to keep the world safe, elements of that safety hinged on secrecy and the ability to get the job done.

Even with that conviction, Trace's words had haunted her in her quiet moments since.

Undercurrents.

Although she'd fought him mightily at the time, she'd felt them, too. And had continued to feel them more and more as time passed.

"The place hasn't been the same since Roger retired." *Or since you left.*

She wanted to say that part, too, but their kiss was still too fresh on her lips. And the raw emotions that came from admitting to herself just how badly she wanted him kept her from saying anything more.

"Who else was there at the time?" Trace turned the coin over before holding it up. "Who else has one of these?"

"They had a few hundred made for his retirement. Anyone on his team at the time could have one, but he could have shared some with family or friends outside the agency, too."

It was the reality of challenge coins. What started in military organizations now extended well past that to police, fire, EMS. Even universities and sports teams had gotten into the idea of customizing human belonging within a group of people.

In their case, Roger's retirement had generated a coin specific to him and his team, honoring his many decades of service.

She'd accepted hers with pride and knew Trace felt similarly about the one he'd received.

But there was something about this one, left right here for them to find, that sent a message.

"You know as well as I do this wasn't left here by Roger's family or his friends."

She stared up at him, the lips that had so recently kissed her, taking her back to a place that still ached in her heart, suppressed into a flat line. Rigid.

And telegraphing an anger she could feel sparking off him.

"No, Trace, this isn't by accident. Someone's sending us a message."

"Which means this isn't just about Brigante. And following you here, finding you here? With me? That wasn't an accident, either."

Deep down, Nic had known that from the start. Was that why she was so invested in this? She'd told herself it was about a child, and that fact remained absolute in her mind, but there was something more.

Something dark and rotten from the inside.

"I was careful. I kept my search for you out of work computers and off the grid."

"Then someone already knew where I was and figured I was the first one outside the agency you'd come
looking for."

"Why would anyone think that?" she pressed, an oddly
sinking feeling settling in her stomach. "We were discreet.
No one knew about us."

That dark, haunted look on his face faded, replaced
with a layer of humor she knew wasn't actually about
anything funny.

"What's that look for?"

"People knew."

The roiling in her stomach dropped clear down to her
feet, a gaping pit. "Like hell they did."

"Nic." Trace shook his head before moving closer. He
settled one hand on her shoulder while the other moved
up to cup her cheek. "For someone so street-smart, you
really do miss the forest *and* the trees sometimes."

"What's that supposed to mean?"

"Roger warned me off of you before anything even
started."

"He never said anything to me."

"He didn't have to. You weren't the one looking at you.
I was."

Even as those words arrowed straight to her heart, a
big part of her struggled to believe it was possible. Did
everyone really know about them?

It struck hard, the idea that people had watched them.
Had known about their intimacies.

And yet…it dropped a few more pieces into place.

"Was that why you were so reluctant to start anything
with me?"

His thumb brushed the edge of her jaw. "Well, yeah.

You're the golden girl, and I was just the ass who had the hots for you."

"You were a top-notch agent and well respected by everyone who knows you. What you do as an adult in your private moments is no one's business."

That grim smile shifted—morphed, really—into a broad one to rival the sun desperately struggling to cut through the clouds. "People have a funny way of making their own observations all the same. And if it's considered remotely scandalous or interesting that goes double."

"People need to mind their own business," Nic snapped. Hearing the harshness, she could be honest enough with herself to know it was out of embarrassment more than anything else.

"Since they don't, we have to figure out a way forward."

She laid a hand over his, still pressed against her cheek, and saw the reality of what she'd brought here to his corner of paradise. "I'm sorry."

His gray eyes, always so expressive, narrowed at the apology. "For what?"

"For bringing this here. For drawing you back in. For all of it."

"I told you I was in this, Nic."

"When it was about a child, yes. But this is more." Her gaze drifted to where he'd found the challenge coin glinting on the ground before coming back to him. "That coin says this is so much more."

"Then we face it together."

"I'm still sorry. For all of it."

"I'm not. If this is about me or my time at the agency, it's been out there, waiting to strike."

"And I brought it here."

That smile—the heartbreaking one that she still saw in her private moments—flashed strong and true. "There's no one I'd rather face it with than you."

Chapter 10

Garner turned the challenge coin over in his hands before passing it off to Jake.

They all sat around the kitchen table, the lights dim against the darkness now settled outside the window, steaming mugs of coffee in front of all of them. Hogan lay on the small area rug they kept in front of the fridge, where he'd been all day. Making himself at home and claiming his spot.

Trace was oddly glad of it, even if it was going to take a bit of getting used to having such a large presence in the house.

But Hogan had been a sentinel for Jake throughout the intruder's attack. And even now, head on his paws, the German shepherd's eyes kept opening each time Jake spoke.

A unit, Trace thought. A man and his dog. Had they only just arrived the day before?

It's been a hell of a day.

Trace nearly said the words aloud but stopped, instead taking in the dynamics at the table. He watched his brother and his friend work through the implications of the coin, sharing a few theories between them, before allowing his gaze to drift to Nic.

She was one of the strongest people he'd ever met, male or female, so he wasn't worried that she'd wilt under the reality of all this. But he did worry about her.

Most of all, he was concerned she somehow felt this was all happening because of her.

In reality, it was happening because of him. He'd bet his life on it.

Leaving the agency and DC behind hadn't just been about getting away from her. Nor had it been about simply leaving a place that no longer filled him with pride and purpose.

He'd known something was wrong. He'd sensed it in Roger long before the man retired with honors. A sense that his respected boss was doing everything he could to keep his fingers in the dam.

But there were cracks.

The unrelenting pressure to expand their remit and take on more shady responsibilities in reaction to the bad actors in the world. Points Trace understood, yet couldn't fully reconcile with the Mom, baseball and apple-pie reasons that got layered over it.

Murder was murder, and you couldn't change that with a slice of pie.

There had also been a change in the tone of their missions. While espionage had carried shades of gray since time immemorial, their reasons for the missions had become more nuanced.

A *suspected* arms dealer acting badly in the Horn of Africa.

A *presumed* scientist in the Middle East selling state secrets.

An *inferred* connection in South America with a group of local militants and an upcoming political election.

He'd been in the game long enough to recognize that all of the suspicion had a place, but the speed with which they acted on it had become difficult to explain away to himself. A truth that had grown even more challenging when he'd seen their secret actions directly benefiting businesses who operated in those places, from shipping to technology to pharmaceuticals.

Was he jaded? Sure.

Was he still right? Hell yes.

"This was from the man you both worked under?" Jake asked as he laid the coin on the table. "Was he a good guy?"

"The best," Nic quickly asserted before her gaze drifted to meet Trace's. "I'm not backing down off of that point, Trace. Roger was a good man. Is a good man."

"I agree. He's the reason I stayed so long." *Him and you*, he thought as he looked at Nic.

But she didn't need to know that. Even as he suspected his brother was well aware of what he'd held off saying.

"So there's no chance he's behind this?" Jake persisted. "Some inability to actually retire and leave the game?"

"It's a consideration, and running down all angles has to include it," Trace added. Jake's police training and years of detective work would ensure he looked under every rock, and Trace appreciated the perspective.

He also knew Roger Bane.

"But I think it's a consideration to drop way further down the list. We'd be better off thinking through who was on his team during the time he retired and who has an interest in extracurricular activities, using agency influence."

"Anyone come to mind, Nic?" Garner had remained

quiet up to now, and his directed question held more censure than Trace was comfortable with.

He trusted his brother and knew that was returned tenfold.

So why was he swiping at Nic?

Yet true to his belief in her, she held her own, her chin held high and her voice firm and direct. "No one's off-limits, but there's no one who pops for me, either."

"But you came here," Garner pushed. "You sensed *something* if you went outside your own resources."

"That's the problem. It's a sense, but it's broadly distributed."

That was new. What did she mean *distributed*? Before Trace could ask, Jake stepped in, his tone calm. "Walk me through it."

Nic glanced at Trace, as if willing him to keep quiet, before launching in. "I've given you the overview of the Brigante case. The shipping and manifests that don't quite match. The size of the business overall and the suspicion Richie Brigante has friends in low places."

"Right," Garner said as Jake nodded with a "yep" of his own.

"So we've been following it. The moment he moved into international waters and began his work with other countries, it moved into our jurisdiction, even as I argued it belonged with coast guard or even FBI to manage, with us assisting."

It was an interesting angle and one Trace hadn't considered, but Garner was already probing further. "You can make that decision?"

"We can recommend. If the base problem was Brigante putting dangerous cargo on his ships and leaving US waters, coast guard should have a role."

"But they didn't on this?"

"They were the ones who brought it to us," Nic said, her gaze going slightly unfocused as she recounted the work. "I was pulled into a briefing meeting and figured that would be the extent of it for a while. We would agree to share some data resources and any intel we had on Brigante. Next thing I know, the work's being taken over, and I'm on the team working the case."

"How'd the coasties take it?"

Nic flashed a smile at Jake. "They don't call them Bears for nothing. Not well."

Trace took it all in and had to admit he'd let his feelings for Nic cloud quite a bit. The overwhelming emotions of being around her again had ruled the day, and it was only now, with the realities of all they'd faced in less than twenty-four hours, that he had to admit the situation went far deeper than he first suspected.

But it was the interagency battle that said the most.

Sure, there were turf wars from time to time. But people also knew their responsibilities and their roles. A decision this overt suggested someone trying to hide their involvement in the core problem.

"Who made the decision, Nic?"

"That's the problem. I can't find who ordered it. I've dug, and I've discreetly asked, and I've even bitched and moaned about the assignment in hopes of getting some detail. But no one seems to know. Or the ones who do are mum."

"So let me play it back," Garner said, his expression flat.

Trace had always thought of it as his brother's SEAL face. The one that said *don't mess with me*. It hid a lot, Trace knew. Emotions that ran far deeper than Garner allowed anyone to see. And a rapier-sharp intelligence few truly understood until it was too late.

"You have murky leadership now that Roger's departed. Interagency battles that no one seems bothered by. And now, based on this coin…" Garner tapped the table "…the assumption that we've got a rogue agent."

"It looks just like that."

"Well now," Garner drawled, shooting Trace a large, wolfish smile. "Looks like things just got good."

"That's one way to put it," Nic said in as dry a tone as she could manage. Did he think this was funny?

Even as the thought flitted through her mind, she knew better.

Garner had questioned her from the start—and since she'd held a gun on his brother, she couldn't quite say she was blameless—but it still rankled a bit. They weren't playing a game.

And yet…someone in DC obviously was. Maybe she'd be better off looking at the situation through that lens, identifying her next move like a chess piece on a board.

Which made Garner's next retort sting a little bit less. "I think it's the only way to put it. You've got an ogre situation going on here."

"I'm sorry?"

"Ogres. Onions," Jake said.

"Layers," Trace added. "Lots and lots of layers."

Awareness finally registered at the pop culture reference. "This is hardly a children's movie."

"Hardly," Garner said. "But it's still true."

Nic gave herself a moment to gather her thoughts, looking at each man in turn. It was a skill she'd figured out early on, when she was new to the work and trying to make a name for herself in a male-dominated world.

Nic Miles held her own.

Always.

"I want to go out and take a look at the surrounding roads," Trace said finally. "We'll see if anything looks out of order or where there might have been an entrance onto the property. I have a few ideas where they might have come in."

His words seemed to have a quieting effect on his brother because Garner only nodded. "Why don't I take care of calling out law enforcement? I can introduce Jake to the locals in the process."

Jake rubbed his hands with a half smile. "My first day and already meeting local law enforcement."

"Start as you mean to go on, I always say," Garner said as he stood up from the table.

Jake followed suit, catching Hogan's attention from where the dog had settled in front of the refrigerator. He obediently followed, as silent as a wraith other than his nails clicking on the kitchen tiles.

Nic considered all they'd learned up at the sniper's perch and the risks of running around in the dark. The ranch was in the middle of nowhere. They'd gotten lucky earlier, but was it really wise to go out at night without any knowledge of what lurked nearby? "It's dark. Do you really think you'll see much?"

"Doubtful." Trace picked up his mug and took a sip of coffee. "But you never know. We could find something. Or we find nothing and keep on driving to pick up some dinner at the diner. No one will argue with takeout tonight."

"I—" She broke off, unwilling to continue the thought. What was she going to do? Apologize again? Or worse.

Ask him to kiss her again?

When her face grew decidedly warm at the image, Nic recognized it was best to make a hasty retreat. "We can take my car if you'd like."

"The rental?" Trace shook his head. "I hope you don't mind, but I'd rather we looked a bit more incognito in my truck."

"Sure. Of course. Right."

She pushed back from her chair, suddenly needing to get away and regroup for a few minutes. All of it had grown heavy. Almost too much to bear, really.

She'd nearly made her escape when she felt a tug on her hand. Trace had reached for her, stopping her movement. "I just need a minute, and then I'll be ready."

"Take all the time you need."

As the mortifying reality that she was staring at a place just over his head took hold, Nic shifted her vision, her gaze clashing with his.

What she saw there nearly took her breath.

"I'm glad you're here. I'm glad I'm the one you came to."

"I don't know why," she murmured.

"Because you need me, and you came to me." His hand tightened around hers. A soft squeeze of welcome and connection, and so achingly familiar it was a wonder she didn't dissolve into a puddle right there. "I'm glad you did."

She'd never considered herself a woman of vast emotions. Appetites, yes. There'd been a time she was insatiable for him. At moments, even now, she could feel that need echo through her body in harsh, clanging waves.

But emotions? They'd always been her downfall.

She didn't like them. Had never wanted them. In fact,

she'd figured out the only way to survive her childhood had been to ruthlessly root them out and live in a way that didn't allow her emotions to exist.

How humbling to realize Trace had pushed through all that.

Effortlessly.

For reasons that made no sense, a night several years ago filled her mind's eye. It was before they'd become intimate, one of several jobs together that had preceded the fall into their ill-fated relationship.

"Do you remember that night?" she asked. "The stakeout in Budapest?"

"I do."

"Do you remember what we talked about?"

"You told me about the kid whose mom came to school and talked about her work as a chef."

Those emotions she wanted to pretend didn't exist speared through her, piercing internal organs as they zipped around her insides like pinballs.

"Why do you remember that?"

"Because you told me." His gaze searched hers. "And because I got the sense as you were telling me the story that long, boring night on stakeout that you were leaving out a very large part of it."

She had left something out, but she was shocked to realize that *he* knew it. "I told you everything. The way she talked about her job and how she told us funny stories about patrons who wanted weird things or how someone brought a dog to her restaurant in their purse and it got loose, wreaking havoc in the kitchen."

His hand hadn't let go, and his gaze hadn't left hers, and Nic recognized somewhere way down deep that she was well and truly lost.

Because there was no way she could deny what was uniquely and innately *them*. No way she could deny how he saw her and heard her and touched her and…just how she felt when she was with him.

"What were you holding back?"

"How much I wanted that to be my mom. This was before the Bakers when I really didn't have anything beyond three squares and a rotating group of foster parents." She closed her eyes against the memory, not even sure anymore why she'd brought it up. "I wanted that to be my mom so badly. To have someone who told funny stories and who came for me at school and who hugged me when it was all over."

"Why didn't you tell me that part?" Trace asked, his voice husky. "Seems like it was the most important."

"That's the point I'm trying to make. I deliberately left it out because I have no interest in feeling that way. Emotions are poison. I don't want them. I can't do them. In fact, I sort of suck at them."

She tried to tug her hand back but he held firm.

"I don't think you suck at them."

"That's because you want in my pants."

"Perpetually and eternally. But news flash. I've been in your pants. I still don't think you suck at emotions." He stared up at her. "I can, after all, keep two distinct thoughts in my head."

The intimacy—one that had nothing to do with sex or nakedness—embarrassed her even more than the frank talk. "I don't do this. So can you just accept that it took a lot for me to come to you?"

His hand dropped away from hers and something shuttered, shadowing those deep gray eyes. "I know it took a lot." He stood then, towering over her but not touching her again.

Nic felt her pulse trip at his nearness. At the way that deep gray seemed to see everywhere at once. The way that gaze seemed to simply envelop her.

"Just so you know, that goes both ways."

"You expect me to believe you've spent the past two years pining for me?"

"Believe what you want, Nic. I know what I know."

And then he was gone, slipping from the kitchen and leaving her standing there staring into space.

The pressure of the case.

The long, exhausting days of searching for a child.

And now this.

Her living nightmare, having to confront all the feelings inside she'd long believed buried.

Or worse.

Admitting she was full to the brim with emotions she'd believed herself incapable of having.

What in the ever-loving hell was wrong with him?

Trace left that question to marinate as he prepared himself for the trip out to the edges of the property, well aware he needed his full focus to go hunting for a killer.

You expect me to believe you've spent the past two years pining for me?

The fact that he almost said yes was proof his head was not where it needed to be.

In the game and totally focused on catching a killer. That's where he needed to be. Especially after their discovery of that little clue up on the ridge.

The challenge coin haunted him, and he knew Garner

and Jake had similar responses. A challenge coin meant something, most specifically belonging to a team.

A unit.

Hell, Trace and Garner had discussed creating a few of their own once they made the decision to move to Liar's Gulch and set up the training facility. Old habits died hard and all that. But both of them innately understood what it meant to belong to something bigger than them.

Which was why that discarded coin packed the exact punch its owner intended.

Trace knew how a challenge worked. A person carried the coin on them so they could hold it up when someone called for it in a social setting, initiating a coin check of the members present. It was both a game and a very real test of emotional commitment.

He still had every challenge coin he'd been given. Most professionals he knew were the same.

So the purposeful discard of one had several messages layered through it.

The person shooting at him and Nic *knew* them.

And they no longer cared to be a part of the team.

Trace finished pulling weapons, ammo and a few other supplies out of the cabinets in the stables and walked into the office for one last check on the cameras. Jake had flagged several points when he was watching the recordings earlier and had encouraged Trace to watch them before heading out. The man might be new, but he was quickly making himself invaluable. Trace appreciated the immediate willingness to help.

He also appreciated the keen eye the seasoned detective brought to the work. An eye that had encouraged him and Nic to get out of the house before Garner called the local cops to help with the body.

Settling himself at the keyboard, Trace ignored the distinct unpleasantness that filled him, knowing there was a dead body not that far away. Distractedly, he wondered if it was bad for the horses. None had seemed worse for wear when he came in and greeted them down the line, but was he risking equine harmony in his stables with this?

Since there wasn't anywhere else to put the guy, they were going to have to risk it, but Trace was anxiously counting the minutes until they had the body off the property.

The videos were queued as promised, and Trace played the first three, each showing the same span of time from different angles. It was only when he got to the fourth—showing the same time stamp and a view on the farthest edge of the property capturing the road into town—that he saw Jake's intention.

Because right there, about forty-five minutes before the incident out front, was a large black SUV barreling down the road. The windows were tinted, but Trace was able to make out two distinct forms in the front seat through the windshield.

It wasn't much, but it was something.

He rewound the tape, the angle of the camera only capturing the license plate for the briefest moment. Even with that quick slip of time, Trace could see the plate had been covered over with mud.

One more indication they had the vehicle of the intruders, if not the identities.

It wasn't ideal, but at least they'd have an image to show police. One more element in their favor when they also produced a body, one who just happened to get himself shot dead on their property.

Trace left the recordings queued where they were for when Garner and Jake walked the local sheriff through the details and picked up his stuff to leave. He had a renewed sense of purpose, even as he knew it was highly unlikely they were going to find anything.

The ridge had been clean before, and Trace had no doubt that was by design. The only clue they were meant to find was the challenge coin.

It was just their sniper's bad luck that he and Garner had been paranoid enough to set up far-perimeter cameras at the very edges of the ranch. Their video strategy left way too much acreage uncovered—it would be impossible to do otherwise—but in moments like this he was grateful they'd thought that far ahead. At least they had a set of eyes on anyone's approach.

He was briefly tempted to rewind the tapes even further and see what Nic's approach had been that morning, but he didn't have the time. Besides, based on where she'd found him in the woods, he likely wasn't going to find it; her hike into the back of the property was inaccessible by the local roads.

Trace was already wearing his Kevlar as he bent to pick up the rest of the items he'd collected and headed for the stables. The material was thick against his body, and he realized it had been some time since he'd had to suit up like this.

A stray shot of adrenaline zipped through his system at being on an op again, a map of the property filling his mind's eye as he shut off the office lights.

The horses whickered a loud greeting, the notes slightly discordant as they filled with restless overtones.

It should have been his first clue.

It might have been if he hadn't had the simultaneous thought that the sniper would have had the same training as Nic. So why did the intruder drive past the ranch instead of come in through the woods the way she did?

A flash flared at the edge of his vision as a blend of instinct and training had him dropping to a crouch, but it was too late.

Something hard slammed against his head, and the pain consumed him as the world went black.

Chapter 11

Nic finished pulling her things together. Her gun. Her two clutch pieces—another pistol and a wicked knife that fit against her ankle. And last, another suit-up in the Kevlar.

She'd given herself five minutes while Trace gathered what he needed in the stables, but she still felt like she was moving underwater.

Slow and ungainly.

And shaken.

It was the *shaken* that pissed her off, but instead of focusing her movements into quick bursts of speed, she couldn't seem to keep her thoughts in any one place.

Why had she brought up that stupid story from school?

To this day, she'd never understood why she told it in the first place. If she were honest, she wasn't even quite sure if she could remember the zigzagging discussion that had gotten them to that point in the conversation.

But stakeouts were often endlessly long and boring to boot. If you were lucky enough to have a partner you liked talking to, the conversation could go anywhere.

Theirs certainly had. From Budapest to Moscow to Cape Town, they'd worked well together and fallen into an easy rhythm. One that had been surprisingly easy to tap into today.

Souls know each other.

Her foster mother, Lucy, had said that frequently. She'd thought it a sweet statement, but Nic had never quite believed it until she met Trace. But once she had? Lucy's sage wisdom had made a tremendous amount of sense.

"You're not soulmates. Or twin souls. Or any other fanciful notion that dances through your mind in weak moments," she whispered fiercely to herself, ignoring the twinge that hit just below her breastbone.

Even if Lucy Baker was one of the wisest—and best—women Nic had ever met.

Instead, she gathered up her things and headed for the living room. A quick glance at her watch showed that despite the treading water feeling, she'd gotten all her stuff together in just shy of five minutes, after all.

It was only when she hit the hallway to the living room that all hell broke loose.

Hogan started barking like a madman, racing toward the door in leaps, his frantic howls and snarls focused on one thing: getting outside.

Jake ran to let the dog out, but Nic raced past him, already reaching for her weapon. Since Hogan was already creating a ruckus, she didn't bother to go easy, screaming as she followed the dog. "Trace!"

Heavy footsteps pounded behind her, Jake and Garner already following, but Nic was beyond caring. She had to get to Trace.

The dog headed straight for the stables, his frantic barking meeting nothing but resistance at the closed door. Up on his hind legs, Hogan pawed to get in, but the large sliding door wouldn't budge, even once Nic got there throwing her weight against it and dragging on the slider.

"Why is it locked?" Garner shouted as he got there, slamming a fist against the door.

"Is there another way in?"

"Back, but—"

Whatever else he had to say faded in the air as Nic headed around the far side of the barn. She trusted the protection around her midsection but slowed as she neared the back side of the barn.

Was there only one other person?

Two?

Had the sniper come back with a partner?

Gun in hand, she moved along the side of the stables, her back to the structure. She paused, doing a quick sweep of the area, before continuing on.

With deliberate steps—and the hope that the barking dog would drown out any noise she might make—she moved around the corner, only to see someone racing off in the distance, a body over one shoulder in a fireman's carry.

Trace!

Or was it the body?

Uncaring, she took off again, positive she could take him down based on the increased load he carried. That had to work in her favor.

It was a good plan. A sound plan, one she was armed to take on and trained to handle.

Only her plan was no match for the trip wire that she ran straight into, falling to the ground as a cacophony of explosions lit up the night sky.

The man breathed hard as he ran with the body over his shoulder. The mercenary had been expendable, but he was still a liability, even dead, so he'd circled back to pick up the body.

Besides, it was fun to match his wits against his old friends from the agency.

Even more fun to show them how outmanned they were.

He kept up the grueling pace, a testament to his training and his own personal fortitude. But even with the hundred and ninety pounds of deadweight, he wasn't going to get caught.

He'd made sure of it.

The little trip wire had been fun to rig, and the small batch of explosives tied to it would keep them busy—and moving more carefully—to give him ample time to get away.

What was more fun was letting them know their small corner of Nowheresville, Wyoming, wasn't safe from him. Hell, he'd spent three days here, and he'd gone undetected. But that was the price you paid for choosing a damn ranch to live on in the middle of nowhere instead of keeping your ass in a city.

Because there was no place, no matter how remote, he couldn't find. And if you were separated from civilization, it made his work that much easier to manage.

His nickname hadn't been Bloodhound for nothing. He had the natural skills of a hunter and the tenacity to hunt down his quarry no matter how long it took.

And Trace Withrow had been enemy number one for a long time.

He'd bided his time on getting his revenge, but Nic Miles had been the key to putting his plan in motion. After she'd interfered in his work with Brigante, he'd known it was time to make his move.

And she'd made it all so easy.

The car he'd driven into town was parked just where he'd left it, hidden in brush on the back side of the property. With efficiency born of working in the shadows, he tossed the dead mercenary in the trunk and slammed the lid.

In moments he was heading for the lonely stretch of highway that led out of this wilderness. He'd stop just shy of Jackson Hole where he'd already stowed another car and all he needed to get out of here and hang for a few days.

He had to hand it to Richie, the guy had delivered on the tools to do the work. It was one more aspect of their partnership that had proven rather fruitful. He erased the man's deeds from the agency databases and got a very nice cut in exchange for the work.

What he hadn't banked on was the sister. The woman was a piece of work, and he was already spending far too much time thinking about her. She was a distraction, but now that he'd put his plan in place, he could lie low and turn his attention toward her. Get her to shake off the old dude she was hanging with and spend some time with someone who could satisfy her baser urges.

Yep, he thought as he hit the highway, he had it all planned out.

Just as soon as he doused the car with gas and the body inside of it, he was taking a few days for himself. Working off a bit of energy was just the thing to get him limber and loose and ready to finish up his plan.

Because Trace Withrow was going down.

That little hit on the head was just a preview of how well he worked in the shadows. When he came at Withrow again, he was going to make damn sure of two things.

Withrow would know who was after him.

And he wasn't going to wake up next time.

Spikes hammered into his skull as Trace struggled to open his eyes.

The first thing he heard was the frantic neighing of the horses, followed by the equally frantic barks of a dog.

They had a dog?

The hammering continued, even as he knew he needed to get up—to move—so he struggled to open them as he rolled over. Something fell off his chest and brushed his fingers, but he had no idea what it was, nor could he fully open his eyes to find out.

And then he didn't care as a wave of nausea rolled through him so hard he nearly blacked out. It was close, but he caught himself before falling straight back against the hard floor of the stables, just rolling to the side before he hit.

"What the—" His words faded off before a harsh expletive spilled from his lips as memory returned. On a deep breath, he opened his eyes and willed himself to sit up, nausea be damned.

It was a close one, Trace had to admit, as he struggled to sit up and worked desperately to keep the contents of his stomach. With a hard inhale to steady himself, he suddenly became aware of the heavy drafts of air coming in through the wide-open back door of the stables.

He hadn't come in that way...

The large spotlights on the back of the barn lit up the land beyond it, and despite the blurred vision he couldn't quite blink clear, he could make out a figure running in the distance. Staggering to his feet, he headed for the door.

Was it the person who'd hit him?

The urge to sit back down and close his eyes nearly won until something in him dimly registered the running form.

Nic.

What was she doing? Why was she running outside? Why was…

Nic!

Clarity returned with all the finesse of a freight train slamming into his skull, but he ignored the pain as he realized it was Nic racing through the property out beyond the barn.

Had she found the intruder?

He took off, determined to keep moving, even as his legs trembled with the lack of equilibrium and the pounding in his skull.

"Trace!"

Garner's large form suddenly filled the space in front of him, his brother's arms going around him to hold him steady.

"Whoa, buddy. Stop."

"Nic. She's—"

"I know. Stay here, and I'll follow her."

Trace pushed against his brother's arms, not quite sure why he couldn't break Garner's grip, but that tight hold moved him toward one of the stalls.

"Hold on here and don't move. I'm following her and will bring her back."

Garner's form wavered before his eyes, but Trace nodded. "Go."

He should follow. He needed to follow. But the best he could do was hold on to the stall door and give his brother room to move.

It was only as Garner cleared the wide-open door that the sky beyond lit up like the Fourth of July.

Vision be damned, Trace took off at a run.

He had to get to Nic.

Nic spit out a mouthful of dirt and struggled to get to her feet. She'd missed the trip wire and had gone down hard. Her puffy oversize coat and the Kevlar broke her fall, thankfully preventing too much damage with all the padding.

It was the fireworks display that was even more jarring than the trip wire.

She recognized it for showmanship—the smoke still lingering in the air—but the bright lights had already faded without leaving any fire in its wake.

Showmanship and diversion, she amended to herself as she got to her feet. Especially because the figure she'd followed—the one weighted down by a body—was nowhere to be seen.

"Nicola!" Garner ran up to her, his gaze skipping past her and all around them. "Are you hurt?"

"No. Where's Trace?"

"In the stables. Dude took him down with a nasty hit to the head."

She didn't wait to hear any more, just took off and circled back the way she'd just come. Even from a distance, she could see Trace come stumbling out the back of the stables, his movements exaggerated before he lost his footing.

The sight of him tumbling to the ground spurred her on, and she dragged off her coat as she ran, dropping to his side. "Trace. Are you all right?"

The spotlights mounted on the back of the stables filled the area with bright light. She used her coat as a makeshift pillow and was careful to lift his head. Only after she had him settled could she see how disoriented and foggy he was by the blown pupils and unfocused gaze.

"I'm fi…" The word slurred off into a hiss as he squinted against the bright overhead light.

Opting not to argue, she bent over him to shield him from the glare. "Is that a bit better?"

"What happened to you?"

His words came out like *wazzz hazzen yew* and didn't do much to make her feel better, but she kept her voice calm and measured, not wanting to confuse him. "A trip wire and some fireworks. I'm fine. I wish I could say the same for you."

"I'm fi…"

Once again his words faded off, and she fought the rising concern that there was something really wrong with him.

"Can you sit up for me? Slowly," she added when he jerked impulsively to sit up. Keeping a firm hold, she pressed one hand to his shoulder while the other went behind his neck to gently help him up.

Trace shot her a dark glare, which she took odd solace from. If he could process enough to be irritated at the question, it meant he was making more connections in his head than his condition might suggest.

He struggled to sit up, but she only had to help him a little as he got into a sitting position.

Before she could ask him how he was, Trace was asking questions of his own. "Are you sure you're okay?"

The question was a bit fuzzy, the words slightly slurred, but he completed the sentence and was slowly refocusing his eyes on her.

And then Jake was beside her, Hogan at his side. "Let me help you."

"Keep the dog here. I hit a trip wire, and I don't want him to do the same."

Jake looked at her for a moment, an immediate kinship springing up at her concern for the dog, before he gave Hogan a few commands. The dog's training was impeccable, and he remained close, following behind them as she and Jake managed to help Trace to his feet, each of them taking one of his arms around their neck.

"We can get him to one of the chairs in the office. It'll give him a chance to resettle a bit before we try to get him to the house."

"I am walking. I can make it to the damn house." The words came out in a snarl, but once again, Nic took heart that each was distinct and layered with irritation.

"Let's try the stables first anyway," Jake said. "We've got work still to do in there."

Realization dawned, and Nic let out a heavy exhale as they crossed the threshold of the stables. "He got the body."

"Yeah, he did." Jake nodded, his mouth set in grim lines as they headed toward the office. "Left a little present this go-round, too."

"Another challenge coin?"

"Yep. I left it on the ground for you to see before touching it."

That sense of being toyed with ratcheted higher—hadn't that been the very definition of all that had happened today?—but she held back the ire and the frustration. There'd be plenty of time for that later.

Right now she needed to focus on Trace.

They settled him into a chair at the extensive console. It had a high back and a place for him to rest his head while she looked at him.

"I cleared the barn," Jake said. "No one else is here."

"While I think we'd all love a shot at him, I'm not surprised," Nic said. "This was one more attempt to stage things according to his own plan."

"You see that, too?" Jake looked at her over the top of Trace's head.

"I'm afraid I do." Nic kept splitting her focus between Jake and Trace, working through what was in her head even as she worried over Trace's injury. "Which now makes me certain Olivia's in even more danger than I first thought."

"How so?"

"The one point that's eased my mind up to now is that she's with family."

"Presumably she's still with family," Jake pointed out.

"Her uncle's a pawn," Trace piped up, his voice clear even as his eyes remained firmly closed. "Whoever is doing this is using Brigante to his own ends. Once he outlives his usefulness, the uncle's in as much danger as the kid."

Nic leaned down and laid a hand on Trace's cheek, the move so like his gentle touch earlier. "Look who's joined the land of the living."

"It was a close one." He smiled as he opened his eyes. "Too close."

His large hand came over hers, holding her in place. "Bastard's playing games. We're going to use that to trip him up."

She heard the conviction, even through the groggy tone. Oh how she wanted to believe him. But they'd been played every step of the way so far.

And since she wasn't even sure who they were playing against, it was impossible to know what their next move should be.

* * *

However many ways Trace had imagined Nic in his bedroom—and he'd imagined plenty—sitting beside him on the bed and holding an ice pack to his head hadn't made the cut.

"How are you feeling?"

She'd asked him the same question at least every five minutes for the past hour, but the aspirin had finally kicked in, and he could at least give her a slightly more honest answer than *fine*.

"The ice pick has dulled down to a ball-peen hammer."

"That doesn't sound entirely promising, but it's improvement, so I'll take it."

"I really am fine. And I'd like to be out in the kitchen with Garner and Jake as they talk to the sheriff."

"They have this covered. You're staying here."

"Bossy much?"

"Grumpy much?"

Even though it hurt, he couldn't hold back the smile. "I can hold the ice pack myself."

"Fine."

Despite the irritation in her voice, she placed his hand gently on the pack before letting go of it and standing up to move around the room. She'd already dimmed the lights, using only a small lamp in the corner that he rarely, if ever, turned on, and it left the room bathed in a golden glow.

"We'll get him, Nic. I promise."

"He planned this. Down to an escape plan out behind the stables."

"He did."

"He's been on your property for who knows how long. Moving around and creating chaos. Hell, if Hogan wasn't here, I don't know how long you'd have been lying there in the stables."

"You would have come looking for me."

Even with the softer light, he'd kept his eyes at half slits, but opened them fully as he watched her storm around the room.

"I shouldn't have had to come looking for you. None of us should have. Whoever the hell this is shouldn't even be here. He wouldn't be here if it weren't for me!"

Although Trace had expected this—and her unnecessary guilt—the explosion still caught him a bit by surprise. Not for its intensity but for the obvious upset she still carried.

"Come over here."

When she only stared at him, he patted the place beside him that was still warm from where she'd sat ministering to him. "Please."

Her cheeks were flushed, and he could see her chest rising and falling from the frustration, but she did as he asked, moving over toward the bed. She even sat without any further coaxing.

Without giving her time to pull away, he took her hand and linked his fingers with hers. "You didn't bring this here."

"I did."

"No, Nic, you really didn't. This situation with Olivia might have brought it here and now, but this storm was coming. Those challenge coins are proof of that."

She'd picked up the second one in the stables—the one the bastard intruder had left on Trace's chest—before they headed in the house. Trace had looked at it before setting it down on his end table.

It was another retirement coin, this time from a col-

league who'd started in the agency with Roger, Stewart
Gaines. He wasn't as respected as Bane, nor was he as
adept at playing politics, but he'd been sent off into retirement with a proper goodbye and gratitude for his years
of service.

And now his challenge coin had been left behind.

The message was clear. This was a vendetta.

"You can keep arguing with me, but if I hadn't come
for your help, this wouldn't be happening."

It hurt to shake his head, but he did anyway, determined to make his point. *Willing* her to understand.

"Don't you get it? Other than my brother, there's no
one else on this planet I'd want having my back besides
you. And if it wasn't this time and place, with you here, it
would be another, without you here. Can you stop blam-
ing yourself for a minute and understand that?"

Although he didn't miss the clear skepticism that had
her shoulders set in hard, tense lines, he saw a few shots
of understanding light up her gaze.

"I need you, Nic. Olivia is our focus. She has to be. But
finding her also means cleaning up whatever is haunting
me from the past. Whoever wants to see me go down has
obviously wanted that for some time. You and I are going
to work together to make sure that doesn't happen."

He wasn't sure if he'd fully gotten through to her, but
in that soft light he sensed that something had changed.

One more shift in the give-and-take between them that
had been happening all day.

From the way they'd started just this morning—and
God, was it only this morning?—to this very moment, it
had been a slow yet determined weakening of the walls
between them.

And defenses be damned, he wasn't willing to fight it anymore.

With that only thought driving him, Trace reached up and laid a hand at her neck, pulling her gently forward for a kiss. He sensed the briefest moment of hesitation just before their mouths met, but it quickly vanished as their lips came together.

Warm and needy and wanting.

Oh how he wanted her. How he'd never stopped wanting her. And in this stolen moment, he was determined to show her just how much he'd missed her.

With soft, aching slowness, his tongue lined the seam of her mouth, teasing her, tasting her. On a soft sigh, she opened for him, her tongue meeting his in blending so carnal he physically ached.

He'd dreamed of her, and he'd longed for her. Both far more often than he was comfortable with. But he'd never believed he'd see her again. Never imagined, no matter how wild the fantasy, that she'd be in his arms again.

So in this moment, with the reality far better than he'd ever imagined, Trace took the precious gift that had been given to him once more.

And vowed to himself that he wouldn't discard quite so easily what had willingly come back to him.

Chapter 12

She was falling.

Deeper and deeper, and she didn't care.

Further and further down the path where memory met reality and would leave her with a whole new set of decisions to make.

No matter how much she'd denied it or believed herself strong enough to resist him, there was no force on earth that compared to what she felt for Trace.

So she'd fall.

And hope like hell she would find her feet again someday.

All while fervently hoping that day was far, far away.

Trace's hand settled at the back of her neck, his thumb lightly stroking the skin beneath her ear. It was erotic and gentle all at once, and she shifted, bringing their bodies in closer contact as she leaned into him.

On a hard groan, his free hand came around her waist, and he pulled her fully against him where he sat half-propped up in bed.

It was in that place, in a half sprawl neither of them were in any rush to move from, that she heard the hard knock on the door, followed by Garner's deep voice.

"Trace, we just got word that—"

Nic scrambled to sit up at being caught, even as Trace's arms still wrapped around her in a tight band.

"Trace!" she hissed, pulling against his hold until she finally wiggled out in an ungainly move that nearly had her falling off the side of the bed.

"Nic." Garner nodded his head. "I'm glad you're here, too. I need to talk to you both."

If he thought anything about finding them in such a position, Garner didn't say, but she didn't miss the twinkle that filled his eyes and had his mouth tilting in a lopsided grin. "I'm sorry it can't wait."

"No, of course not," she said as she smoothed down her hair, taking a few discreet steps away from the bed. "What's going on?"

"Jake and I've been briefing the sheriff. While we were talking, a report came in about a car torched about fifteen miles outside Jackson Hole. With a body inside the trunk."

Trace sat further up on the bed, his expression sharp and holding steady as he moved. Nic moved closer, holding his arm to help him up.

"Maybe we should go talk to the sheriff then," Trace said, looking at her. Despite the tightness of his features indicating he still had some pain, there was a clearness to his gaze that had her breathing a bit easier.

Was kissing restorative? Were raging hormones a strong counterpoint to a likely concussion?

Tamping down on *that* line of thinking, she just nodded. "Maybe we should."

"How do you want to play this?" Garner asked. "I gave him the base information but haven't expanded on Nic's involvement or the possibility that we have a rogue federal agent running around the wilds of Wyoming."

Nic had braced for this possibility from the start. While

she'd come here with the expectation that she could handle the mission, local law enforcement being none the wiser, she'd also run the scenarios if the opposite happened.

It looked like the thirty-four percent probability she'd calculated was more likely than she'd given it credit for.

"May I take the lead?" she asked.

Garner tilted his head, something that looked like acceptance and appreciation in his eyes. "The show's yours."

Since it was, Nic made her excuses to slip from the room and headed for the one she'd been using. Might as well pull her credentials from the start and make every effort to play nice with the locals.

Technically she had the advantage as a federal agent, and she knew it—and the sheriff would, too—but she wanted this to go smoothly. For this case and for whatever Trace, Garner and Jake needed in the future. Add on that she was here on her own devices and technically without supervisor approval, and that only made the whole thing murkier.

Best to go in with a smile and an air of collaboration.

Less than twenty-four hours in Trace's company, and you're already working outside the lines.

The thought would have been funny, she realized as she pulled her badge out of her bag, if the stakes weren't so high.

Nic headed down to the kitchen, which had proven to be the heartbeat of the house, and found a man who looked as lean and mean as Jake only with Garner's height.

"Hello." She extended a hand. "I'm Nicola Miles."

"Sheriff Dawson Kane." He maintained eye contact, but she didn't get the immediate sizing-up feeling. Oh, she had no doubt he was taking his own impressions, but he was damn good at concealing the fact that he was.

"Sheriff. Good to meet you."

"Life has certainly gotten interesting since the With-row boys moved to Cage County."

"You flatter us," Garner joked as he came into the kitchen, his hand on his brother's elbow. Although Trace was doing a decent job of holding his own, Garner kept close watch and did help him into a seat at the table.

"Trace." Dawson nodded.

Trace's greeting was equally simple. "Dawson."

Goodness, they'll be grunting next, Nic marveled to herself before taking the empty seat beside Trace. "I'm afraid what I'm going to share is going to ratchet up the interesting scale."

Dawson remained impassive, but his hazel eyes were sharp and laser-focused on her. "Please go on, Ms. Miles."

"Nic will be fine."

"Nic, then."

"I realize I'm putting you in a difficult position, but I'm going to start with asking you if you could consider keeping this to yourself for a few days. I understand if you can't, but I believe once you hear the full story, you may consider my request."

Although Dawson had remained fairly unflappable since they'd sat down, she saw her words made a dent.

"I'll tell you how I came to be here and the reasons why we think trouble has followed me."

"What sort of trouble?"

"Kidnapping and murder, Sheriff Kane."

Nic had brought a hell of a lot more than kidnapping and murder to Cage County, but Trace held his own counsel on that as she launched into her story for Dawson.

From her initial suspicions in DC to her search for Trace to the contact with Olivia, she shared it all.

Garner and Jake added in context about the intruder and subsequent movement of the body and offered to take Dawson out to the front porch as well as the stables so he could get a few photographs.

Nic wrapped up the story with what they assumed was the sniper returning to retrieve the body and the attack on Trace, as well as the trip wire on the run to the woods.

"That takes some time to set up. And it suggests he's been on the property," Dawson hypothesized.

Trace hated the reality that they'd been unaware of an intruder, but he couldn't argue with the facts. "It does."

"I'm happy to send a few deputies out to help you cover ground. I don't lie to my men and women, but for now I'd be comfortable saying you had an intruder, and we're looking to understand where they might have hid out."

"We appreciate that."

Dawson nodded, and it was as good as done.

Trace respected the sheriff and knew the man was good for Cage County. Dawson had dealt more than fairly with him and Garner since they moved to Liar's Gulch and had supported what they were looking to do.

Yes, they had military and covert skills, their decades of training too valuable to fully waste, and they wanted to put them to use selectively helping those in need. But they were also committed to their horse-training-and-rescue business. Jake had come to the ranch committed to the same after leaving the Las Vegas PD.

It was "what came next." That change in life stage that began to haunt him a few years before he officially left the CIA. Garner had experienced it in the SEALs as well, though his was a bit more tied to the physical rigors of his job and the reality that no matter how well he was trained, his work had a shelf life.

The horses—a path Trace had never anticipated for his life—had brought passion and a purpose that meant something. He no longer depended on higher-ups or missions or the ambitions of others to rule his days. Instead, he worked with animals whose only purpose was to live day by day.

The work had centered him. Given him a new focus for his life. And hell, he just plain enjoyed it.

Which made the fact that he'd sunk back into his former life so easily something of a surprise. And, if he were honest with himself, a bit of a concern.

He wasn't that man any longer. Even if today had made it clear that life seemed to have other ideas.

"This is quite a case, Nic. You think Brigante's operating here in Wyoming?" Dawson asked.

Trace keyed back into the conversation, the extra set of eyes something they couldn't underestimate.

"I think he's farther north, lying low in one of the border states. My money's on Montana, but it could just as easily be South Dakota or Idaho."

"You don't know?"

Nic had been open and honest with Dawson, and she didn't veer off that course. "He's been to all three states in the past three months."

"Staking out territory?" Dawson probed.

"That's what we don't know. Brigante runs a legitimate shipping business. There's every reason he could be in any of these states, setting up contracts for warehouse space or legitimate contracts to move goods across the border."

"But he operates in New York. Why come this far west?"

Nic grinned, the look triumphant, and Trace didn't miss how Dawson sat a little straighter at her bright smile.

"That's part of what has us concerned. He could just as easily move goods through upstate New York or Pennsylvania or Ohio. It's suspicious, especially since he doesn't have any business outposts in the Pacific Northwest."

Dawson paused, considering all Nic had relayed. It was one of the qualities Trace respected about the man. He was thoughtful and he listened, two traits that made him good at his job.

"Tell you what. I'm willing to give you seventy-two hours before I file my notes. You could keep me from doing anything if you had a mind to, but you've dealt fairly with me, and you've kept me informed. I can give you that in return and hopefully keep you off the radar of anyone with prying eyes in DC."

"I appreciate that, Sheriff."

Dawson's attention shifted to Trace. "You took a pretty hard hit today. How are you feeling, Withrow?"

"I've downgraded from ice picks to the skull to hammers."

"Improvement, but not enough to go running around. You want to think about calling in a doctor?"

"I'll take it easy and up the aspirin dose."

"Why'd I get the feeling you were going to say that?"

While Trace appreciated the sentiment, his vision had cleared fully and he was no longer seeing double. And the hammers had dulled to a steady throb, even easing up as the medicine took hold. He was fine.

"And why do I get the feeling no one's taking it easy?" Dawson continued.

"We need to see this through," Trace said. "I was committed before someone came onto my property, tried to hurt all of us and got the jump on me from behind. It's personal, Dawson."

"That's what I'm afraid of."

Nic chose that moment to stand up, effectively ending the conversation. "You've given us seventy-two hours. I intend to use every minute of it. Thank you."

She exited the same way she came in, gliding out and presumably heading for the guest room. Each man watched her go, but it was Garner who spoke first.

"I'm shooting straight with you, Dawson. I was the first one to give her a hard time, but this mess is way beyond her. And she needs all the support she can get."

"And you, Trace?" Dawson said. "You think she's on the up-and-up?"

"Yeah, I do. We worked together a long time. And whatever's really going on here, I think they've made Nic a pawn to get to me."

"Who'd you piss off?" Although Dawson said it with a smile, there wasn't a trace of humor in his voice.

"Hell if I know, Sheriff." Trace shook his head, using the pain to fuel him. "Hell if I know."

Olivia spent a sleepless night, worried about the hacking computer call she'd made to Nic. It didn't seem like anyone had figured out she'd done it, especially since her uncle and his friends, Jane and John, had basically ignored her all day.

But it was their absolute lack of interest that had her wondering if she'd done something stupid by reaching out.

She trusted Nic, even if she didn't like that she hid stuff. Well, Nic didn't hide things the way her mom did. It was more that Nic hid some bigger reason why she wanted to keep Olivia safe but didn't want to tell her what was so dangerous.

Olivia didn't actually think her mom or her uncle

would hurt her. They were stupid adults, but they were her family. But she really didn't like their friends.

Even with all that, had she overreacted?

She'd been on her best behavior, only coming down to the kitchen for lunch and a soda in the afternoon. Her uncle was on his phone like always, and when she asked about John and Jane, he told her they were running errands.

What was dangerous about that?

Since no one would tell her where they actually were, she had gotten busy after lunch hacking the Wi-Fi. You couldn't get an exact address off a router, but it had given her some basic details. She did get the provider, and it was a local service available in the northwest, mostly in Montana, based on a quick search of their coverage map.

The whole dude ranch thing didn't really seem real, but a walk outside hadn't shown much but an empty stable and an old chow house with a dated kitchen and long rows of tables. It seemed odd that the ranch part was so run-down and the main house was so big and beautiful, but it was one more thing no one wanted to explain and she innately knew she shouldn't ask about.

Jane finally came back late in the day, but John wasn't with her. Jane did bring a few frozen pizzas back with her and made them for dinner, but it was so quiet as they ate that Olivia decided to tell them about her explorations for the day, telling Jane how cool it would be if she and John fixed up the dude ranch and held weddings here.

Jane didn't seem that impressed with the idea, but Olivia really played it up, making up a big story about how her mom could be their first bride. That at least got a laugh out of Jane, but it was sort of a mean laugh, like it was a joke instead of something that could happen.

Olivia just pretended she didn't hear the mean part and

said that she was going to her room to work on a business plan and mock up a website.

It gave her something to do—not that it was real—but she was bored, and it also meant no one would pay a lot of attention if they found her on her computer.

But she kept worrying about the fact that she'd called Nic. Would she come try to find her? And if she did, what would happen?

It really did seem like they were on a dude ranch, visiting friends of her uncle's. The main house was big and elaborate, and the rest of the property was run-down, but it wasn't like anything else was happening.

Olivia loved her computer and knew how to occupy herself, but she was sick of being cooped up and couldn't even get excited about playing around on the computer for another day. Maybe she'd ask Uncle Richie if they could go somewhere or head into whatever town they were in or just… It didn't matter. She was bored, and she wanted to do something.

Wrapped up in her thoughts, she nearly walked into the kitchen when the sound of voices stopped her. Uncle Richie and Jane were yelling, and there was a third voice, but it was too deep and low for her to hear.

She briefly thought about ignoring it—adults yelled all the time—when she heard her uncle shout, "You killed John!"

"Shut up, Richie!" Jane shouted. "We talked about this. About what had to happen."

"You never said you were going to kill him."

Olivia didn't stay to hear the rest. Whatever feelings had her messaging Nic the day before came flooding back, making her stomach hurt and her mouth water in fear.

Something bad was happening here.

When she heard heavy footsteps inside the kitchen, someone pacing around, she stepped backward, keeping her own footsteps light.

Quiet.

Even once she was out of earshot, she walked softly, not wanting anyone to hear her.

It was only when she got back to her room that she grabbed her computer where she'd stowed it under her pillow and pulled up the VoIP calling program she used. She'd never called Nic before, but she had already saved her number in the program in case of an emergency.

If someone was dead, this qualified.

Nic was part of something big. Olivia had always known that and had always feared being traced or tracked because of it.

But now?

She needed help.

And somehow knew that Nic was the only one who she could turn to.

Trace was still pondering the question of who he'd pissed off the next morning as he tried to ignore the light flooding his room. It was muted and gray—the impending snowstorm looking more and more like a done deal—but it was still daylight.

And the headache he'd managed to get under control the night before protested.

Mightily.

He hadn't expected to fall asleep, assailed as he was by tortured images of what he and Nic had been doing in his bed before Garner's interruption. But the hit on the head as well as the exhaustion of the day caught up to him and he'd fallen asleep almost immediately.

After a quick shower and another handful of aspirin, he managed to feel semi-human. A cup of coffee and some breakfast might go all the way toward getting him back to the land of the living instead of feeling like an invalid sent to his room.

Trace figured he'd eat and then quickly run through morning chores feeding and exercising the horses before diving back into the Brigante case. He needed to check if Olivia's mother had taken the bait on the text messages, and then they needed to map out a plan for finding Olivia. Hopefully spying on Eloisa's texts would give them an idea of where to find the child.

And if there was an ex-colleague lurking behind it all? They'd deal with that when they got to it.

The scents of coffee and breakfast meats hit him as he walked into the kitchen and found Nic at the stove, spooning something out of a large casserole dish.

"Good morning."

She turned with a bright smile, and he was taken aback, the domesticity of the moment hitting far harder than he'd have expected. "Good morning. Hungry?"

She'd always been an early riser and claimed that breakfast was her favorite meal. Something he'd seen firsthand when he would sleep over and wake up to the scent of her cooking something.

Nic Miles wasn't a bowl-of-cereal or a cup-of-yogurt eater, either. Eggs were nearly always a part of what she made, and she actually cooked things to go along with it. Bacon. Sausage. Sauces if she was feeling extra creative.

"I made a breakfast casserole. Garner and Jake are out feeding the horses and will be back in soon."

Trace tried to shake off the memories and get his head

back in *today*, but he couldn't quite regain his equilibrium. And it had nothing to do with getting hit over the head.

Garner and Jake had taken the final feeding last night, too, after walking Dawson through the crime scene. Garner's expletive-filled don't-mess-with-me response when Trace had protested that he could help had been enough to keep him inside, but now here he was stuck again— eating eggs fraught with memories, and Nic flitting around his kitchen like some goddess of the morning, bright-eyed and ready to take on the day.

Was he the only one who'd been affected by last night's kissing in bed? Or *on* a bed, he amended. He dumped sugar into his coffee, sloshing the hot liquid over his hand as he dragged the mug off the counter.

"Damn it!"

"What's wrong?" Nic was by his side in an instant, but that only seemed to fuel whatever irritation gripped him like a too-tight pair of shoes.

"I've got it. Just clumsy." He marched over to the counter with his coffee, running his hand under cold water before wiping the mug dry. Couldn't even get his damn coffee in order.

"Are you having headaches this morning?"

"Hell yes, I'm having a headache."

"Sit down and let me look at your pupils."

Although neither of them were trained physicians, they had received basic medical training before being sent out in the field. Enough to make basic diagnoses or understand things to watch out for on routine injuries.

"I'm fine, Nic."

"Sit. Down."

She took his mug off the counter before he could grab

it and walked it to the table, him following along like she was the damned pied piper. Dancing to her tune.

Wasn't that his lot in life?

It was only when he was in a chair, her leaning over him, that he realized his tactical error.

He wasn't concussed.

He was in love.

Had never really been out of it. He mentally regrouped as the reality of it all came crashing in with far more force than last night's blow to the head.

"Look at me. How many of me are standing here?"

"One."

She bent closer, an exercise in torture as his body tightened uncomfortably with her nearness. "Your pupils look good."

"Pupil dilation isn't a reliable sign of concussion."

"It's not wildly off base, either," she muttered as she held his face in her hands, her gaze searching his. "And you fumbled the coffee mug, which concerns me."

"I'm fine, Nic."

He heard the warning notes in his own voice, but for some reason she didn't seem to, her gaze still searching. "Do you have any eye pain or any sensitivity to light?"

"No."

"Did you sleep last night?"

Would have slept better if you were with me. Only he didn't say that, opting instead for, "Like a baby."

"What about stiffness?"

"Damn it!" He pushed her hands away, standing up. Was she messing with him?

"Trace! What is wrong with you?"

"You can't be that oblivious." He stalked back over to the counter, putting distance between them because he had no other idea what to do. He wasn't going to beg for her attentions, and he certainly wasn't going to get into her personal space if she didn't want him.

"What the hell is that supposed to mean? Oblivious to what?"

"Us, Nic! You and me. Together. We were interrupted last night, and then I was sent to my room to sleep like a child. But us is what I'm talking about."

She stared at him from across the room, the initial shock that rode her features changing—morphing, really—until her face crumpled into hysterical laughter. "I actually asked you if you were stiff!"

Before he could register what was happening, she'd doubled over, dropping into the chair he'd just leaped out of. "And…and…" Another fit of convulsive giggles took her over.

"It's not funny." He might not want to be considered a truculent child, but even he heard the whiny notes in his tone. Damn it to hell, what did this woman do to him? Why was he reduced so quickly by the simplest things?

He might have even asked that question if her phone hadn't vibrated on the table.

Nic's eyes went wide as every bit of laughter died in her throat. "It think it's Olivia."

"Answer it."

Even from across the room, he saw her hands tremble as she picked up the phone.

"Hello?"

He watched Nic's face, the humor nearly all gone.

"Where are you, Olivia?"

Whatever the child was saying wasn't audible to him, but he could see Nic getting more and more tense as she scribbled notes on a pad left on the table from earlier.

He moved closer, eyeing what she wrote down even as he itched to hear the conversation.

THINKS MONTANA WITH A COUPLE SHE'S
NEVER MET BEFORE.
NEW ARRIVAL AT THE HOUSE.
ANGRY UNCLE.

Trace considered the notes, curious when Nic underlined *angry*. What was Richie angry about? Had he figured out Olivia was communicating with Nic? Or had something else upset him?

"I'm coming for you. I—"

Nic pulled the phone away from her ear, staring down at the face, the home screen still lit up. "She's gone."

"What did she say?"

"She's gone, Trace. I don't know where she went, but she was talking to me, and then her words just stopped."

Trace saw the swing of emotion and the way fear rapidly took over her thoughts. "Call her back."

"The connection was bad. I don't think it was a standard cell phone."

"May I?" He extended a hand, and she gave him her phone, the calling app still open. He redialed the number, putting it on speaker and getting nothing but a ring. Over and over it pealed through the kitchen, no one answering. After ten rings, he tapped it off and focused on her notes.

"She's in Montana?"

"She thinks so. She hacked the Wi-Fi, and the router owner is a regional provider."

He filed that away, aware it would be hard to use a utility as a resource, but it was information. "What else?"

"They won't tell her where they are. She's been smart

enough not to keep asking, but all they keep saying is how great it is that they're at a dude ranch. There's a couple there with her and her uncle."

"Names?" He kept firing questions, trying to pull out whatever information she'd gleaned from the call.

"Has to be fake. John and Jane Smith. She said she found out the husband is dead, and there's a new man there at the house."

Trace avoided a sarcastic remark on the originality of the names and kept firing the questions. "Did she see him?"

"I don't know."

"A new guy and a dead guy." When she only stared at him across the table, Trace pushed. "We had a sniper and a dead man here yesterday. If she is in Montana, he's had all night to get there."

"What are they doing in Montana?"

"Border access. There's a crossing about seven hours north of here into Alberta."

"Why would they use a major crossing?"

"They may not be hiding anything yet. But they're setting themselves up for it. Setting up patterns of coming and going."

All things they would need to set up a proper smuggling business.

What didn't play was Olivia. Why involve a child, no matter how precocious?

But it was Trace's conviction that gave her the boost she needed.

"Let's go find her and get her back safely. Then we take them down."

Chapter 13

The border-crossing angle made sense. As did the sniper and the dead man. What didn't make sense was Olivia.

Nic went over it and over it as she loaded up her gear. Trace had already gone to update his partners, and they'd agreed they would start on the road, running whatever they could on their computers while Jake and Garner worked the same from home base.

She'd overheard some stern words as Trace fought with his brother about Garner's loudly stated view that he and Jake should come along. It seemed like Trace won the day—especially when he pressed the fact that the ranch was breached the day before, and someone needed to guard it—but Nic figured it was a close call that there weren't four of them heading out of Liar's Gulch fifteen minutes later.

"I can drive."

Nic glanced over at Trace, not at all surprised by his mulish expression. "You're operating on a likely concussion. I'll drive for a while, and you take over in a bit. It's probably not great for you to stare at a phone, either."

"I loaded up on aspirin. I'm fine."

"We'll agree to disagree." Before he could argue, she pressed her point. "We have no idea what is waiting for us on the other end of this drive. You were injured yesterday, and it makes sense to conserve as much energy as possible. I need you to have my back."

She'd like to believe it was her reasonable tone that had him agreeing but suspected it was the risks of the sobering reality they faced.

"I get it."

Since he did, she couldn't resist teasing him a bit. "And I know you hate it when I drive, so put one in the win column for me."

"I don't hate it when you drive."

"You do, but I never really knew why. You're not normally a sexist pig, so what is it with the driving?"

"I'm not—" He broke off, and there was something in what he didn't say that hit her with all the force of a lightning strike. "It's stupid."

She had no idea why she was pushing it, but there was something in his tone, and they had a long drive, and well…it was Trace. "I'm sure it's not."

Trace didn't say anything for quite a while, and she gave him his space. He might be a hard and often unyielding man, but he'd never dismissed her because she was a woman. Nor was that unique to her because they had a relationship. She'd always seen him equally forthright and collaborative with all their female colleagues.

"The last time I saw my mother, she drove Garner and me to our grandparents' house."

Whatever she expected him to say, something about his mother was nowhere on the list. She'd always suspected he'd had a difficult childhood by virtue of the fact that he avoided the topic. Since hers had carried more than a few challenges, she'd always given him that measure of privacy. But now she had to wonder if it was one of the reasons they'd bonded the way they had…if there was something they each recognized in the other.

"So it's not about you or your driving," he finally said after a long stretch of road had passed.

"How old were you?"

"Eleven. Garner was nine."

"I'm sorry she did that."

"It was a long time ago."

"It doesn't make me any less sad for those two boys in the car."

She didn't have to look at him to see the wry smile on his face. "Yeah, well, those two boys channeled it all into being big, strong men. Who knows what we would have been if she hadn't dumped us."

"Was life with her bad?"

"She wasn't particularly stable in her child-rearing. My dad took off when I was three, but I was too young to remember him. I don't know a whole lot about him, but I do know he was found dead a few years later, so no looking for a reunion with dear old dad when we got older."

Nic let him talk, the joke about her driving somehow releasing a dam of memories.

"I don't know that they had a great relationship, but it was enough to give her a measure of stability. And raising kids is hard in the best of circumstances with a partner who's there with you through it all. I think there was one day where she just broke."

"And your grandparents?"

This time, she heard the real smile under his words. "Gigi and Pops are great. Were great. We lost them a few years ago, within six months of each other. But they were the best. Real. Solid. Pops is who taught Garner and me to fish and ride horses and love the outdoors."

"And Gigi?"

"She's probably the biggest reason I respect women with as much awe as I do." He turned to face her, and she risked pulling her gaze from the open stretch of road to look at him. "She didn't take any crap from either of us, but she showed us love every day. She did her damnedest every day to show us that we mattered. And she was a seriously kick-ass lady. She hunted and fished. Dressed her kills, too."

"Impressive."

"It was. And it wasn't just the nature stuff. She had a wide group of friends and was part of the community. She wasn't a great cook, but she was an awesome baker, so there were always cookies in the house. She was—" He broke off as if trying to find the right words. "She wasn't just a great woman, she was a great person. And it took me a long time to realize just how important it was that Garner and I saw that. And lived it with her."

It did make Nic wonder if his mother had done him and his brother a service in the end. As if parental abandonment could ever be a service to anyone. Yet even as she considered it, she had to admit that she felt the same about herself.

She'd hated foster care but ended up okay. The Bakers had made sure of it. But even without their steadying influence, she'd developed her own moral compass and had always felt she would have found her way. She was forever grateful she didn't have to know if that were true but felt it all the same.

And if she'd stayed with her parents? Whoever they were? She might not have ever gotten any of that. The Bakers. Or the future. Or her own sense of self.

It wasn't anything you could have proof of, but she'd

come to a place over the past few years where she'd found a level of acceptance she could live with.

Trace spoke again, and her heart cracked a little bit more at the blend of strength and vulnerability threaded through his words.

"I always sensed Gigi was disappointed her own daughter hadn't stood up for us. That she'd found it easier to walk away than to fight. But she never said it. Never left Garner or me with any words that would burn into our memories and ruin our mom."

Nic reached for his hand, laying hers over the back of his where it rested against his thigh. He didn't brush her off, which she took as a good sign.

Along with the fact that he'd decided to say anything at all.

It was a hell of a lot more than she knew about her own parents, but it was interesting that both of them had found their way into adult roles as operatives.

They were both the "type," as it were—individuals who had less to ground them to a family and were therefore potentially more open to risk-taking and the demands of a covert lifestyle.

And yet based on Trace's story about his grandparents and her own experience with the Bakers, Nic couldn't quite take on that idea and believe it applied to either of them. They did have something to lose. They also recognized how precious life was.

It hadn't made her reckless, it had made her determined.

A trait she saw in Trace as well.

"Your grandparents sound like incredible people."

"They were."

"They raised two incredible men, too."

He turned his hand over beneath hers, linking their fingers. "I'm not sure I'd go that far."

With the road ahead flat and empty, she turned to look at him, shockingly full of emotion. "Without question or hesitation, Trace Withrow, I most certainly would."

Trace finished filling up two coffees at the gas station convenience store about halfway through their drive. Black with too much sugar for him and just milk in hers, no sugar.

He still knew how she liked her coffee.

And what she tasted like.

And those soft moans that filled her throat when they kissed.

He *knew* her.

And he'd spilled his guts like some lost little boy who still missed his mommy.

Only...

He slammed the last lid in place and headed for the register to pay for the drinks and their gas.

Only it hadn't felt like spilling his guts. It felt like being honest. It felt like opening a door he'd kept firmly locked to everyone including himself. It felt like healing.

He wasn't quite sure what to do with it. Because she wasn't staying. No matter how quickly they'd fallen back into intimacy over the past thirty-six hours, they'd left each other for a reason.

He couldn't lose sight of that.

The truck was done filling up when he got back outside. Nic had opened the driver side door to wait for him, her head down as she focused on her laptop.

"What are you working on?"

"Garner texted while you were inside. Said he had something for us to consider."

Trace handed her one of the cups before leaning closer as she tilted the laptop toward him.

"The Sweetgrass-Coutts crossing." She already had a web page pulled up that showed the various United States and Canada border crossing stations. "It makes sense if they're in this part of the country."

"That would work. If they're looking for border access, that's the most likely one."

"Agreed. But here's what's got me really going." Nic smiled. "Take a look at what the guys did with the dude ranch angle. Garner's sending me a list of three properties that have changed hands in the past eighteen months. One of them is eight miles from the crossing."

"Looks like my brother and Jake have more mad skills than I gave them credit for."

"I told him to send me the properties, and I'd dig into the actual ownership on my side. You drive while I do that."

Confessions aside, he'd wanted that from the start—to drive and not feel helpless and injured. Take back a bit of control by being behind the wheel.

So why was he still grumpy as hell?

Garner and Jake had helped. Nic had her computer in hand. He had the drive.

"Why are you all squinty and irritated?"

He glanced over at Nic as he came to a stop before turning onto the highway. "I'm neither of those things."

"Sure you are. You want to run this op, and you're irritated we're all taking pieces."

"I'm pissed you're all taking *all* the pieces."

"You're on point for any texts from Olivia's mother."

"Which I checked an hour ago and still nothing."

They'd been using their mobile phones as hot spots, and he'd logged in to the small program he'd written convinced he'd see Eloisa's engagement with the fake text messages.

Only to see she hadn't even opened the text.

Great game he had.

"Pull over," Nic ordered.

"We need to get going."

"Please pull over."

Although the highway gas station was busy, it was a slow enough time he was able to make a U-turn away from the entrance and turn back into the parking lot. Finding a space out of the way from incoming traffic, he pulled back into the lot and put the car in Park.

"What, Nic?"

"What has you upset?"

"I'm not—"

Without warning, Nic leaned over the large center console that separated them in the truck and pressed her lips to his.

The light flavor of coffee met him as her mouth moved over his, and despite his frustration and irritation and all around general pissiness, he caught on quickly to what she was doing.

A spiral of need opened up in his chest, the kiss rapidly spinning out of control as their mouths met, then met again. That soft sigh he loved so much echoed between them in the cocoon of the truck cab. In this moment that was both carnal and comforting, Trace recognized just how well this woman knew him. What made him tick and what drove him wild.

And what smoothed out the rough places inside he avoided with everything he was.

Pressing one last light kiss to his lips, she shifted back into her seat and smiled brightly. "You in there?"

"Yeah, I'm here." He glanced out over the parking lot, his gaze taking in the big wide-open sky beyond. "Yes, I'm upset. About feeling helpless and out of the action."

"You've done so much."

"That remains to be seen."

And it did, but he'd also done work like this long enough that he recognized the value of teamwork and partnership. He was also honest enough with himself to know that wasn't the real problem.

She deserved to know it, too.

With his own gaze steady on that crystal blue that *saw* him, he admitted the truth. "I'm not sure why I told you that story about my mom earlier."

He saw a series of expressions flash across her face, surprised to realize the pity he expected wasn't one of them.

"I'm glad you told me about her. She's a part of you, and that experience is a part of you, and I have to confess, I'm rather greedy."

"About what?"

"I want to know you, Trace. I've always wanted to know you. And that story is you."

"It was a long time ago."

Something shifted on her face, her expression set in the fierce lines of an argument. Which was at odds with the gentleness in her voice. "And you spoke of it like it was yesterday."

"Don't make it more, Nic."

And then fierce shifted whip-quick into matter-of-fact.

"Don't make it less. Whatever you want to say about it now or even if you regret what you told me, don't make less of your feelings or your experiences. Most especially not the ones that made you the man you are today."

It shouldn't have bothered him. He'd shared the most intense moments of his life with this woman, and barring his brother, no one knew him better. And still it all burned, somewhere dark and shameful inside of him.

Those memories of abandonment.

He laid his head back against the seat rest, his gaze continuing to follow that wide arc of sky. "She never came back."

"I know, baby."

"I don't want it to matter. By now it shouldn't matter."

"But it does."

"It never goes away." He turned to look at her, keeping his head against the rest to center himself. And what he saw in her eyes nearly broke him.

"It never leaves you. Whether you can rationally appreciate why those feelings are there or whether you try to dismiss them because of time and distance and life." A few tears spilled over her cheeks as she continued. "It never leaves you, Trace. And maybe on some level, it shouldn't."

"Even if life moves on."

"Because life moves on. But that child doesn't. You will be forever eleven inside, and that's okay. It's what made you an incredible agent. What makes you a man who has the patience and the fortitude to work with horses and give them a new life. It's what's made you the man you are today."

Throat tight, he wanted to keep dismissing it all. Just keep pushing it away with both hands and a shovel if he had to. Yet despite everything inside of him wanting to deny that truth she spoke so eloquently, he knew she was right.

"I'm still not sure why I said anything. I don't think about this every day. That child may live somewhere inside of me, but the man knows how to get up and get to work every day."

She reached for him, once again linking their hands over the console between them before those depths of blue captured him once more. "Maybe you told me because it was time."

Time.

It did its work, Nic reflected as the miles passed by them outside the truck windows. For good and for bad, time did its work.

Her conversation with Trace in the gas station parking lot kept echoing through her head, those moments of raw vulnerability leaving an echo of quiet softness between them on the drive.

Neither of them had said much these past few hours. A few comments about the drive. A quick parry-and-thrust of theories as to who Brigante was working with. A discussion about who they could remember at Roger Bane's retirement party who might have received one of his challenge coins.

Despite those shots of conversation, the two of them had remained quiet, lost in their own thoughts and the weight of what they'd shared.

"What's the end game here?" Trace asked, breaking the silence.

Nic turned to look at him, captivated as always by the solid lines of his profile. There was a strength there, and a resolve that spoke to her on a visceral level. And he was just so damned attractive.

Sheer need filled her, heat flushing her skin.

Since there was nothing to be done for the rash of hormones in the middle of a long stretch of highway, she did her best to mentally swat it away. She could pine later.

More to the point, she mentally admonished herself, she knew she would.

"I know what you're asking but don't get the context. End game for Brigante?"

"Him, sure, but if he's running as many nefarious practices as you believe, his world is already a lot of 'live by the sword, die by the sword.' It's the idea of a rogue agent that I keep circling around."

"Why is he doing it?" Nic clarified.

"Not that I'm excusing it, but the temptation to get a side gig can be explained. But why risk discovery with this showboating? Because if this is about running a side gig with access to Brigante's influence and business, taunting a former colleague is a hell of a way to go about it."

What else *could* it mean? People made bad choices all the time. His mother leaving him and his brother. The criminals the world over they used to thwart together. The scale might be different, but the capacity to do damage was sadly the same.

"Every move so far has been a tactical assault in the vein of a game," Nic mused. "I'm not sure that speaks to long-term thinking and stability."

Trace tilted his head, considering. "Maybe not, but then what was the trigger? You and I have cycled through everyone we know together as well as individually and can't come up with a candidate for those challenge coins. No one even pops a bit as a loner or disgruntled."

"What about triggers? Were those retirements a part of it? Overlooked for a promotion? Passed up for a desired field assignment?"

They could be triggers, but it still suggested a level of instability she didn't understand. Everyone knew the risks in the job. Even those who romanticized the work knew what they risked, especially once trained for the field. Would someone really take that training and use it as a form of vengeance if they didn't agree with something in the organization?

Their earlier conversation drifted through her mind. The difficult childhoods that had made both her and Trace into good agents could be a consideration for who they'd become as adults. Even as she turned that over, she couldn't deny that both of them also found their way to adults who cared for them.

Was that the difference?

Or was there a third piece that couldn't be underestimated, either?

Her college psychology classes had called it nurture versus nature, which she had understood in the end just to be the realities of life and the choices they made every day. "What if it's in their profile?"

Trace glanced her way. "What profile?"

"You know, the idea that organizations seek operatives who have difficult childhoods. Loner personalities. Genius aptitudes. Even those who might have underlying adjustment issues."

"That's been glamorized a bit for entertainment, don't you think?"

"Even if it is, those traits could lead someone to the job. So whether by deliberate design or by personal choice, the work draws people who choose to operate outside the norm."

He was quiet for a minute, and she was surprised to see the emotions that played over his face. As a man who normally held back those reactions, it was humbling to see his willingness to be vulnerable. "Like you and me?"

"This isn't about our conversation earlier, Trace."

"Maybe it should be. Maybe if we acknowledge the vulnerability, we can also wield it."

It was a fascinating idea, Nic realized, catching on to where he was going. Even if she needed to stress the bigger point. "It's still choice, Trace. You and I chose differently, even with less-than-ideal childhoods. People the world over, in all walks of life, do the same."

"You've been in the agency for a while now, and our training is similar, so you'll know what I mean when I say this. Didn't you ever get the vibe off someone that they got more out of being an agent than actually doing the work?"

She could come up with a dozen people who fit that bill. "It's a component of the work."

He grinned. "Probably something you don't hear a lot of from dentists."

"Oh, I don't know about that. Bicuspids can be awfully alluring."

"I'll give you that, but you know what I mean. There's a distinctly different set of motivations here that go beyond greed. *You* came into the job with the conviction to do the work. Whoever is doing this wants the power. That's the dynamic we can't disregard here."

"Which further reinforces that Brigante's a pawn. Useful only until he isn't."

"Which may be soon." Trace eyed the mirror before

drifting to the side of the highway and pulling over. Once stopped, he shoved the truck into Park and turned toward her, excitement lining his features. "That's what we have to find. The escalation has to be tied to the culmination of some big play with Richie Brigante. Our former colleague, whoever he is, thinks he's getting out with a big score, and he's going to take me down along the way."

"Which means Olivia's really not safe."

"No, she isn't." Grim determination carved deep lines around his mouth and eyes. "Getting her out is the first and only goal. Only after we've done that can we push for the rest."

"I think we start with the property Garner and Jake found. The one closest to the border crossing."

"We need to do it in stages. Reconnaissance first." His gaze was deep. "We can't let Olivia know we're there right away. You know that?"

"We can try."

"She's the priority, Nic. You know she is. But we need to know what we're up against. If there's more danger to grabbing her than laying out a plan, we may need to leave her there a bit longer."

She knew he was right. No matter how desperately she wanted that child out of all of this, safely away from the adults in her life, she knew how to run an op. How to take part in one.

And sometimes, heedlessly racing through the door was the absolute worst way to meet the end goal.

"I understand."

And she did. Olivia's life was the first priority.

But she also understood herself. This case had become personal. Both because she increasingly believed that she was some sort of pawn in the home office to get to Trace, and because in order to do that a child had been put in the gravest danger.

This was no longer *just* a rescue op. It was a mission to get data to take down a rogue agent and bad actor in an organization that way down deep she still believed in.

Despite it all, Olivia came first.

If it mean sacrificing her own life, Nic would keep the child safe.

Chapter 14

Trace scanned the various images Garner had sent to him and Nic when they stopped for a quick bite to eat. They didn't dare look at any of this in public, so they'd picked up sandwiches and chips and settled back into the cab of the truck.

The air outside had grown whiplash cold, and the skies had progressively darkened as they drove north. The winter storm that had been promised for nearly a week increasingly looked inevitable, and Trace wasn't sure if that worked for them or against them.

It would offer some additional protection, potentially, as the occupants of the dude ranch weren't as likely to be outside and catch them moving around the vast acreage. But it was a distinct disadvantage if they were traipsing around and got caught. Add on the fact that escape was a hell of a lot easier when the roads weren't blocked by blizzard conditions, and Trace was worried the storm was a factor they couldn't fully prepare for.

With that thought, he weighed the benefits of waiting it out, knowing Nic well enough to understand that waiting was highly unlikely. So they'd plan as best they could and take their chances.

Focusing on what he could control, Trace looked over

more of what Garner and Jake had been up to while he and Nic drove north. In addition to the maps and intel, his brother had already gotten them a room at a small hotel about fifteen miles away from the property they'd prioritized—the one eight miles from the border—and Garner had done some additional digging into the deed transfer.

"The property changed hands ten months ago."

Nic swallowed a bite of her sandwich, something thoughtful settling in her eyes. "I was put on the Brigante case about nine months ago. Coincidence?"

"Never was a big believer in them myself."

She smiled before taking a sip of her soda. "Me, either."

They continued to bat ideas back and forth. He still wasn't convinced Nic wasn't going to prioritize Olivia above all else, and he got it—he didn't like the idea of leaving the girl in that nest of vipers, either—but they'd deal with it when they got there.

On some level, a part of him wanted her out of it. If Nic rushed Olivia away, he could get down to brass tacks with whomever their rogue agent was knowing both of them were safe.

He took a bite of his own sandwich, well aware of his own personal irony. Since she'd arrived on his property, worried over this child, Trace was concerned Nic had let the op become personal. And now here he was, considering facing whatever this was all by himself if it meant Nic was safe.

"It looks like there's the main house and several outbuildings we can use for cover." Nic stilled.

He knew what she was thinking. "What if they have dogs?" Trace was transported to the same memory. "Moscow?"

"Yes. I still have nightmares about those guard dogs."

She shivered. "But the point stands. Dogs or not, there's no way they're in the middle of nowhere, planning whatever this is and leaving themselves open without some sort of security."

"We'll plan for any eventuality. Luckily we're in beef country, so we can pack a deterrent to bring with us."

"Adding it to the grocery list."

It was amazing how easily they fell back into it. The exchange of ideas. Each of them taking on various responsibilities so that they maximized the time they had to plan.

It was easy.

And just like those memories of their close call in Moscow, it was something they shared. Those common experiences that bonded them in ways he hadn't fully realized until she came back.

"I'm glad you found me."

Nic paused typing up the grocery list on her phone. It took a heartbeat or three before she looked up and met his gaze. "I'm glad I found you, too."

"I know we left things in a bad way, but I need you to know I never wanted it to end that way." He took a deep breath. "Even though I take full responsibility for my part in how it ended."

"I wasn't my best self there at the end, either."

"I insulted what you believed in and what you stand for. I was in the wrong."

And he was. However much anger he'd left DC with, the time since had given him much-needed perspective. The reality of it all was that he'd equated his relationship with Nic to his job, and when he blew up one, he hadn't known how to preserve the other.

It was his biggest regret.

But now that she was back, he couldn't help but feel

like he had a second chance to make things right. "I know I hurt you, and I'm sorry."

She nodded, swallowing hard around what looked suspiciously like tears. But it was her quiet acceptance that nearly did him in. "I'm sorry, too. Sorry I couldn't see my way to where you were at or why you were so done with it all."

"How could you know if I refused to tell you?"

He knew he didn't have a right to touch her, but oh how he desperately wanted to change that. Not just be worthy of her again but to find some way forward.

Some way past all that came before.

It made no sense, and the two thousand miles that stretched between their lives only reinforced that.

But a man could dream.

And he could burn from the wanting.

With all that clamoring inside him, he pressed a hand to her neck, gently pulling her toward him to press a kiss to her lips.

It was chaste and gentle, but he felt its impact clear through his entire body.

Because if he was lucky, it was the pathway to washing his soul clean.

Nic saw the change in him as much as felt it. A strange sort of acceptance flowed between them, connected by their lips but, as she well knew, connected by so much more.

For better or worse, Trace Withrow was the catalyst of her life.

There was who she was before him and who she became after, and nothing could change that. Not even the way they ended things had managed to change her steadfast belief in him.

The question was if they could get past all that had come before.

It was only when he pulled back, his gaze soft and full of a yearning that would likely have weakened her knees had she been standing, that she pressed for more. "Tell me about it. Tell me what happened to drive one of the best field operatives out of the organization."

He took a long sip of water, but it seemed more in preparation for the discussion than stalling.

"I saw what they were doing. The guise that it was all in the name of being the good guys, yet it was hard to see where we ended and the bad guys began."

The ops world had an endless number of shades to it, and she accepted it when she went into the field. But... if she were honest, she could also acknowledge what he was saying.

When the work had purpose and clear lines that were being crossed by an enemy, it made sense. When it seemed a bit more opportunistic, she'd chafed a bit. And whether it was because more of the work was becoming opportunistic or because she'd been at it long enough to understand, she hadn't yet figured out.

"It's a difficult line to figure out because the edges are so soft."

"Are they?" The question came out as an edgy laugh, but she sensed what he meant.

"At times, I do think that's true. But at others?" She couldn't deny his point. "I agree with you."

"Well, I had one with edges so soft they were squishy. Right before you and I met. We had to get intel for one of the SEAL teams to take out a wannabe dictator in a small African nation."

"Someone who could have done damage," Nic said.

Yet even as she pointed it out, she recognized the reasons for his underlying anger and disillusionment. "But let me guess. The dictator angle wasn't great, but his ascension to power would put a key shipping channel in danger."

"Called it. It's one thing to take someone out for human atrocities and genocide, but someone who potentially wanted to control waterways that his country had genuine rights to?"

Nic did understand. And while she'd been sheltered from something quite as questionable as Trace's experience, she understood why it had disillusioned him.

"That was the third op in a row where I spent more time questioning what I was doing than simply acting. I knew my job, Nic. I understood my role and also understood in many ways I was a tool to get a job done."

"You're more than that. We all are."

When he only stared at her, his gray gaze so cold and bleak, she remembered part of that last fight between them.

You think this is about any of us? That they really see any of us as truly valuable?

Of course they do. Why else would we be trained as elite operatives, able to get in and out of any situation?

We're expensive tools, nothing more. Don't fool yourself, Nic. There is nothing keeping us safe except for each other.

Nic had shuddered at his attitude at the time, but she'd be lying if she didn't admit how often those words crossed her mind in the two years since. How that assessment—as stark as it might have been—had felt more and more real as she went through her assignments.

Expensive tools.

And now they were going up against someone who likely matched the same description.

"But you used that term…before," she finally said. "Tools. A means to getting a job done."

"And I was okay with it for a long time. I figured if I understood it, I could handle what came my way. For quite a while, that attitude worked just fine."

"Until it didn't."

"Until I woke up and realized that I wasn't a tool, I was a weapon."

Nic busied herself in the refrigerated meat section of the grocery store Trace had found about five miles from their hotel. Although she wanted nothing more than to go straight to the property Garner had shared with them and nose around, she recognized the benefit of regrouping and taking stock of their assets.

And picking up plenty of attack-dog deterrent.

She'd already hit the pharmacy area and picked up an economy-size bottle of extra-strength sleep aids. It was crude, but it would hopefully do the trick, especially when stuffed deep inside balls of ground beef.

If, you know, there were dogs.

Meanwhile Trace worked through the rest of their list. Food supplies for the next few days, several large packs of bottled water and some easy-to-carry trail food, depending on how long they needed to stake out the property.

What each of them seemed to tacitly understand yet didn't voice was the need to double whatever they were purchasing because of the unpredictability of the storm.

The conversations they'd had that day continued to roll through her mind as she picked up a few more food items. From a basket of fruit—portable energy—to a trip down the snack aisle for the canned potato chips she and Trace both had a weakness for, those conversations ebbed and flowed through her mind.

The story about his mother had hit a deep chord, but it wasn't unexpected. Sad to be sure, but a reinforcement of the story she'd pieced together in her mind. Trace's deliberate shift of conversation each and every time they talked about his parents had always left her with the assumption that something unfortunate had happened there. Now that she had the specifics, those long-ago conversations made sense.

What hadn't been quite as clear were the demons he carried over the work.

Until I woke up and realized that I wasn't a tool, I was a weapon.

Was that really the work? She'd believed they were doing what was right. What was noble, even.

Was that belief all a lie?

Because while she understood his point of view—and didn't excuse the missions that had left him feeling that way—she couldn't look back over more than a decade of her own work and feel it was meaningless or in service only to underhanded or shady objectives.

Nor did she think, for a minute, that she hadn't made a difference.

And it wasn't just looking back and trying to make herself feel better. From an international human trafficking ring that she'd help dismantle to a cybersecurity protocol that had protected banks and utilities and schools to other missions that had made the world a safer place.

It mattered.

But his experiences mattered, too. And it was that perspective that…

She nearly bobbled the can of chips she held as the implication of it all hit her.

"Nic?"

She looked up from picking up the chips to find Trace, his concerned expression at odds with the triumphant feeling coursing through her.

"I think I might know what's going on. Or have a theory at least."

Although the aisle was empty, he looked around before stepping in to push the cart. "Did you get everything? Let's get out of here and talk about it."

"Yeah, I'm good."

He looked at the chips in her hand and shook his head before reaching behind her and snagging two more cans. "Now we're good."

Fifteen minutes later, they'd paid for it all and were heading toward the hotel. Snowflakes had started swirling as they loaded the truck and fell steadily as they drove, one of the chip cans open between them in the cupholder.

"What has you so excited?"

"You. The conversation we had earlier."

"We had a few."

"I'm sorry about your mother. About what her leaving did. But that's for us." When he risked a look her way, she added, "Just us."

"All right."

"I'm talking about the work. The experiences you had. Oddly, even taking it back to the fights we had. You and I were on the same team and didn't see eye to eye about the work. Or our purpose."

"We had a shared purpose."

"But different perspectives." Again, Nic realized this was her chance. If not to make things right, at least to make the two of them whole again. "Not wrong perspectives. I don't think that or feel that anymore. I'm sorry that I ever did."

His phone dinged just as the GPS indicated their next turn, and she half thought he might answer. But he only took the turn and waited for her to continue.

"What if the person we're looking for had one of those perspectives? Was somehow at odds with their management or was on an op that broke them somehow?"

"And that excuses it?"

"Not at all. But it does give us a place to start looking. A person with bad intentions and whole lot of rage can do a lot of damage."

"We've been through the list of people who'd have those challenge coins. No one fits."

No one did fit, and that was the other problem. Add on sniper-level marksmanship skills and a sizable enough build to fireman-carry a dead body, and they were looking for someone who was *noticed*. Someone with a physical presence and a set of skills his fellow operatives would understand to be valuable.

"There's no one I can come up with, either. And I saw him. The back of him as he ran from the stables last night, but I did see him."

"What do you remember?" Trace turned into the parking lot of the hotel Garner had booked. The property had hotel suites and would give them an opportunity to spread out.

"He was a physically large male. Which is important because he not only lifted the dead guy, but he ran with him, too." She let out a harsh expletive that earned a grin from Trace. "I would've caught him, too, if not for that damn trip wire."

"He was prepared."

"Bastard."

Trace pulled up under the portico and put the truck in Park. "Let me run in and get the keys. It'll be less notice-able if I go in, and then we can finish this discussion in our room." His grin widened before he leaned forward and pressed a hard kiss to her lips. "I love it when you talk dirty."

"That wasn't talking dirty. It was just a few swear words."

"I'll take what I can get."

Before she could say anything else, he was out of the truck and heading inside to complete their check-in. She watched him go, the simple act of being with him and talking things through making her feel less alone.

Hadn't that been one of the worst things about him being gone? There had been many, but it had dawned on her a few months after he left just how much she missed having Trace in her life.

Yes, the sex and the intimacy absolutely. They were incendiary together and had been from the start. But it was so much more than the physical.

She missed *him*.

The way he knew her and listened to her. The way they bounced ideas off of one another and never really got ir-ritated with each other. The way they could just sit and be with each other, not needing to fill the spaces with conversation.

One of her favorite memories was of a day they'd spent walking the monuments in DC. They'd started early, cups of coffee from a street cart near her apartment in hand, and just roamed. The Lincoln Memorial to the World War II Memorial and all the other amazing stops along the

Reflecting Pool. They'd held hands as they stared at the soldiers that made up the Korean War Veterans Memorial, and she'd felt...connection.

Looking at those statues, just larger than life-size, still and yet suggesting movement all the same, she'd had an overwhelming sense of belonging that she'd never felt in her life.

Those statues and the culmination of the monument captured the reality that freedom was not free. Her work epitomized the same. And she had a partner who understood that. Who understood her.

That had been one of the hardest things to understand about their fights over the work, because they really didn't fight about anything else. They were oddly compatible and in tune with each other. Other than a minor irritation or terse comment from time to time, they got along and worked well together.

But in the end, it was the work that brought them together and the work that tore them apart.

A police SUV drove through the hotel's portico, pulling her attention from those memories that had been so close to the surface these past few months. The driver had a large brimmed hat on, low over his head, but she got the distinct sense he was keeping watch all the same.

It was...

It was a small-town patrol, she reminded herself and sat back in her seat. She briefly considered flagging him down and sharing her credentials, but just like speaking with Sheriff Kane the night before, bringing in law enforcement put her on the radar. Here and back home, because there was no way any cop worth their weight wasn't going to run her and then get curious and call back into DC.

She didn't need that.

Even if it would be nice to know she and Trace had some backup.

The cop kept driving, his arc through the portico slow but steady, and she dismissed the thought of asking for his help. If they needed resources, they'd find a way to ask for it, but now wasn't the time.

But it didn't escape her notice that the cop stopped once he cleared the portico, his gaze on Trace as he came back to the truck with the keys.

Nor did she miss the way he kept his gaze on them when Trace followed that same arcing path to the parking lot to find a spot.

That thought about reaching out for local assistance flared again, and she considered getting out and flashing her badge to set the right tone. But before she could make her move, the cop moved on and headed for the exit.

"He was watching you?" Trace asked as he unpacked the cold groceries and put them in the hotel suite's refrigerator.

"You going to keep being paranoid about this?" Nic asked from where she was logging in on her computer across the room.

"A local cop stares you down, and it doesn't bother you? It's not paranoia."

"Okay, fine. When he looked the first time, I didn't think about it. The second, when he watched from the parking lot, I did reconsider."

"Reconsider doing what?"

"Going over and flashing my badge. Introducing myself and telling him we might need help."

Trace restrained himself from slamming the fridge door, but it was a close thing. "Why would you do that?"

"Why'd you call in the local sheriff at home? We're two people, and we have to get a kid out of a situation we have no intel on. Trained backup isn't a terrible idea."

Trace trusted himself, and he trusted his instincts, and her description of the cop made him itchy. Why the hell was the man looking at them? A cursory glance, protecting his town and all that crap, fine.

But to look again? To focus on them? It didn't settle well, and he knew better than anyone it hadn't settled well with Nic, either. So why was she trying to brush it off?

"I had to wage war with my brother to get him to stay behind and keep watch on the property and any other problems that might come to the house. He'd have gladly come along. Jake, too."

"I already brought one civilian into this. I don't need to drag in two more."

"We're not civilians."

"Yeah, Trace, you are. I know that chafes a bit, but you don't have a badge or a federally supplied gun or access to top-secret information any longer. Neither does your brother or a former Vegas cop, no matter how well-intentioned."

"So you'd rather go it alone than admit you need their help?"

"I'm trying to keep them safe and avoid any of this blowing back on any of you. You and Garner have built a nice life up here. You have your equine program and your side jobs when you choose to take them on. You've built something good and continue to build on that every day. I don't want my choices to take that away from you."

"We chose to help you. I chose first, but Garner and Jake are all in, too."

Battle lights filled her eyes, but she kept her voice deadly calm and even. "And I'm choosing what I'm willing to accept."

"Damn it, Nic! You don't get to do that." Trace stalked across the living area of the suite. "Why come to me at all if you're going to be like this?"

Before he could say anything else, she was on her feet, facing him down. "I can't take this away from you. What you've built in Wyoming. The life you're living. I appreciate your support and your help and all you've done, but I need to figure out how to keep this on the up-and-up and ensure you don't lose your new life because of me."

"Too late. You don't get to make that choice any longer."

"I'm not going to see you go down again. You left DC in disillusionment. I won't see you lose your business now, too."

"This is about me! Damn it." He shook his head, frustrated that he couldn't seem to get through to her. "Why won't you see that? You've been used in this. They're after *me*. It's revenge against *me*. And I can't sit here and worry you're going to take off on some half-formed idea that I need protecting."

"Are you trying to insult me?"

"I'm trying to make you see what's going on here. And maybe—just maybe—accept the reason you've lost control of this is because it wasn't about you from the start."

Trace hated that the work could drag them back to this place so quickly. Hated even more that they still couldn't seem to find level and common ground for very long when it came to the work.

"I appreciate this display of chivalry, but what I really can't understand is how you've managed, in twenty-four hours, to make a case I've been working on for nearly a year all about you. You, who raced away to live in the far reaches of the Western wilderness, a lifetime away from DC and office politics and the agency, are somehow important enough to generate all this."

"Because it is about me. It's about someone gunning for me." God, how did he make her see this?

It was like every bit of progress they'd made before they started out for Montana had vanished, replaced by the by-the-book woman he believed had faded in favor of the realities of the op. Had he been that wrong?

Or had something changed her mind?

"The murder on my property yesterday wasn't about you. Neither are the challenge coins, including one left on my chest, or the mercenary bastard who tried to do damage to all of us. I need you to stop looking at this like a field op and start seeing it for what it is. A twisted game."

"And you're the prize?"

"Yeah, Nic. I'm the one some out-of-control mind has decided has to pay some price. And I'm afraid if you don't get in line and understand this, you've been played harder than I thought."

"Damn you, Trace!" She threw up her arms before turning and facing the window. "We're back where we were two years ago. All about you. What you think. What you claim to 'know'..." she added air quotes "...and the lines you think only you can draw. What about me? What about my life and my career and my efforts? Why won't you give me the proper credit on this?"

And there it was.

The raw vulnerability that suggested she did know—

on some level—what he was saying. But she was bound and determined to fight that truth in favor of all the places where she felt overlooked or overruled.

Or where she had to admit her precious agency could do wrong. Or even worse, could house a traitor in its midst and never even know.

It was that truth that straightened her spine as she turned away from the window to face him.

"The whys of it don't matter, Trace. Don't you see that? I brought the monster to your door. Me. No matter how it happened or if I was manipulated or if it was just a hoped-for outcome on the part of an enterprising disgruntled employee, who knows? But I brought this to you. Can you understand how that weighs on me?"

He took a few steps closer, the ravages of the storm between them fading a bit. "That's why we're stronger together."

"You shouldn't be in it at all."

"But I am in it. I—" He broke off as something caught his attention outside the window. Despite the bright white of the snow that had increased even since they'd been inside, he could see a dark shape moving around in the parking lot.

It shouldn't have registered or mattered, until he realized…

"Hell! What's going on with my truck!"

Nic turned toward the window, her training kicking in apace with his.

Before either of them could head out to confront whoever was messing around with the truck, a wall of sound filled the air. The building couldn't fully withstand the pressure, shaking around them as a ball of fire filled the parking lot.

Chapter 15

Trace raced out of their room, headed for the exit. Nic would have followed but realized he hadn't grabbed anything in the way of firepower, so she diverted to where they'd set up their small arsenal of weaponry in the bedroom. As she picked up two pistols, she sent up a silent thank-you that they'd gotten everything out of the truck.

Even if they were now stranded with no means to find Olivia.

She remembered to snag her cell phone off the desk and shove it into her pocket, along with one of the hotel key cards.

"One problem at a time," she muttered to herself as she followed Trace's path. They'd focus on Olivia after they got this handled.

After...

The parking lot had filled with people, several trying to get closer to the now-smoldering truck to see what was going on. Every last person had a cell phone in their hands, recording the damage.

And Trace stood closest to the burning vehicle, staring at the wreckage.

The sound of sirens was heard in the distance, and

Nic had another flash of that police officer's attention on her and Trace when he'd driven through the parking lot.

Was he responsible?

It hardly seemed likely, but who else knew they were here? They'd used minimal communications, and she hadn't yet logged in to her work VPN. She was about to once they got settled in the hotel room, but she hadn't since they'd left Liar's Gulch.

So who found them?

And why was it only that too-attentive cop that kept coursing through her mind?

Although people were interested, the snow was whipping around all of them in increasing spirals, and it was enough to send quite a few back to their rooms. A few of the phone-wielding diehards stayed, but as soon as the cops and fire trucks pulled in and obscured their view, they headed off as well.

Which left her outside in the driving snow wondering how to play this and just how wide-open she was to discovery.

Even still, a growing voice inside roared with excitement that they'd finally broken something open. This wasn't an accident. She wasn't even convinced it was a message. But she was damn sure it was a deterrent, designed to keep them from getting to Olivia and whatever her uncle was hiding this close to the country's border.

Trace caught her eye as a cop and her partner got out of their vehicle to come closer. She read his intention immediately and came to stand with him, taking a spot under his arm and putting on her most worried face.

"Oh gosh, Officers, we're so glad you're here. Who would do something like this?" She added a soft little moaning wail at the end, pleased to see a shot of sympathy in the partner's eyes.

"It's okay, ma'am. We're going to figure out what's happened here."

"And in the snow that's just getting worse. How will we ever get home!"

Trace tightened his hold, and she recognized the direction to ease up on the histrionics but couldn't resist one last hiccuping sob. When she got another gentle smile from the second officer, she took it as a good sign.

The lead officer asked a series of questions and moved them a small distance away so that the fire department could see to putting out the blaze. Trace answered each question, his answers slow and deliberate and ever-so-slightly misleading.

In the course of the officer's questions, Trace managed to pepper in that they wanted to spend one last visit seeing this part of the country before they moved away for a new logging position he got in Washington. That he'd just proposed on this trip and how awful it was that they were starting their life together with a car fire. And his last salvo was how upset his dad was going to be that he went and ruined his truck.

By the end of it all, the cop asking the questions looked uncomfortable enough to want to wrap it up and the partner had already gathered a few sweatshirts for them from the trunk of the police vehicle to keep them warm. Nic thanked him profusely and the cops shared cards and promised to file a report for insurance.

All in all, the increasing snow conditions did them a favor. There would no doubt be a host of new questions once the truck was towed and an incendiary device discovered somewhere in the chassis, but for now the aw-shucks answers and the increasing snowfall bought them a few days.

Nic stood with Trace's arm around her shoulders, matching shell-shocked expressions painting their features, as first the fire trucks drove away, then the police vehicle.

"Dad'll be right mad, no doubt about it."

The deep voice held distinct notes of laughter as Nic whirled around to find Garner behind them, with Jake and Hogan beside him. Jake and the dog moved on toward the truck, Hogan making a circle around it before stopping midway down the passenger side of the truck bed.

"That's a good boy." Jake fed him a few treats and pointed toward the frame. "You'll find the device under there."

Garner nodded. "We'll remove it in the morning after it cools."

Nic glanced around, pleased to see the parking lot was empty. The driving snow continued to support their desire to remain hidden. "What are you both doing here?"

"You don't think we'd let you two have all the fun, do you?" Garner shook his head as Jake added a "no way in hell" to punctuate the comment.

"Let me guess, there are two rooms booked?" Trace said, his voice dry.

"Three actually," Jake interjected. "I'm not sharing a room with him. Hogan and me need our space."

It was a bit silly, and an odd counterpoint to the fight she and Trace were having moments before the explosion, but Nic couldn't deny she was happy to see them. A new vehicle was essential if they were going to get Olivia out safely.

And she hadn't quite shaken off Trace's words or his

determination to make her see reason. His comments had hurt, but now that they'd just seen the truck explode into a raging fireball, she had to admit there was likely a strong thread of truth to his position.

I'm the one some out-of-control mind has decided has to pay some price. And I'm afraid if you don't get in line and understand this, you've been played harder than I thought.

The backup was welcome.

The additional firepower was welcome.

But the two more able bodies—well equipped to keep Trace safe—were the most welcome of all.

Call Nic.

The small voice that had whispered to her all morning drifted through Olivia's mind once again as she sat stretched out on the couch in the media room watching a movie.

She'd have to be careful about when she made the call, but she could probably do it. Especially if she waited for when she knew Uncle Richie and Jane were hushed off somewhere.

They kept doing that, like no one could figure out they disappeared to make out.

And then there was Jane's husband. Her uncle's *old friend* from college who was dead but no one seemed to care.

Olivia stayed out of their way, and no one seemed to care that she kept to herself, either. But she felt safer that way, and that worried her.

Just like Jane worried her.

The new guy who came yesterday didn't seem to even notice her or see that she was there. He hadn't actually said a word to her. It was Jane who kept looking at her with those watchful eyes.

Suddenly, it all felt like too much.

Why had her mom sent her here? And why wasn't Uncle Richie making a point to spend any time with her? Her father didn't care, only showing up every so often.

Why did everyone *not* care about her?

The tears came hard and fast, and she let them roll. Not like anyone was here in this stupid place to even care.

Not like anyone cared.

Except Nic.

She'd cared from the beginning. Wasn't that the weird part? Someone Olivia didn't know had more feelings for her than her own family did. And Nic meant it, too. Olivia got the sense that something about her own situation was important to Nic, even if she didn't understand why. But Nic had been the only one to believe that nothing in Olivia's life was normal or even felt very real most of the time.

Call her.

Do it.

Call Nic.

The thought had been steady, and it kept getting louder the longer she sat there.

The only problem was if Olivia did call her, she still didn't have anything to tell her. She had no freaking idea where she was, and even if she could figure it out, she didn't get the sense Jane and the new guy would take very kindly to someone coming to pick her up. Uncle Richie might just let her go, but the other two wouldn't.

That she knew with absolute certainty.

Which meant she had to figure out how to get out and get to a place where Nic could find her.

The media room didn't have much in the way of help-ing her figure out where she was, especially since there weren't even windows in here. And the view from her bedroom only showed a lot of land and a ton of trees at the edge of it.

She could try to figure out how to get to the trees. Of course, she needed her stuff. But if she only kept to the essentials of her computer and her phone they still had stashed somewhere and that small piece of her baby blan-ket that she kept stuffed in the bottom of her backpack so no one could see it anyway, she would be okay.

Only problem was she didn't know where her coat was.

Which hadn't seemed like a big deal until she realized that she hadn't worn it since she arrived, and she had no idea where it was.

It was cold outside. Her breath had frosted up the glass in her room when she was looking this morning.

Could she really do anything without a coat or her phone? Because even if she got a hold of Nic and even if she got to the woods, she'd still have to keep going outside.

Coat aside, it was time she figured this out. Olivia needed to get to Nic—that was all that mattered—and she needed information in order to do that.

Since her bedroom was the only thing besides the media room that she was allowed into on this floor—and wasn't it interesting that all the other rooms were locked?—she headed toward the staircase. She couldn't hear anyone, which probably meant—and ewww gross—that Uncle Richie and Jane were making out somewhere. Still, if they were otherwise occupied, it would give her a chance to nose around a bit.

She just needed one item that would tell her where she was. Maybe a piece of mail on the counter or a take-out bag with an address on it or a credit card slip from some-where local. If she got a location, even the city she was in, she *knew* Nic would find her.

The house was so silent it felt eerie and creepy around her, but she kept on. If anyone found her, all she'd have to say was that she was hungry and looking for food. It wasn't like she lived here. If they caught her in a drawer or cabinet, she'd make up an excuse.

Or she'd pull the same routine she saw some of the girls in her class do and just complain that she was bored. Everyone hated a whiny teenager, but they also expected it, so she'd use that to her advantage.

The kitchen was quiet and way too neat—did people actually live here?—so she started with the drawers first. The wall of cabinets was huge so she just went down the row, pulling drawer after drawer. Several were empty, but then she got closer to the sink and the dishwasher and found utensils and one full of spatulas.

Not a bill or restaurant menu in sight.

She'd just hit a drawer that had some junk in it, her hand closing over a magnet for a local pizza place, when the lights flipped on.

"What are you doing in here?"

Olivia's heart slammed her chest and her stomach clenched hard, but she scrambled to hide the magnet in her palm as she came face-to-face with Jane.

Act bored. Act bored. Act bored.

Images of Madison Townley and her group of picture-perfect friends filled her mind's eye, and Olivia did her best Madison impression, hoping beyond hope her voice wouldn't crack. "This place sucks. I'm so bored."

"You have a full media room and a full pantry. Why are you in the drawers?"

"I told you, I'm bored. There's nothing to watch."

"There are about five hundred DVDs in that room."

"Nothing good." Olivia added a pout. "And I've seen all of it anyway. Why don't you have anything streaming?"

Jane's eyes narrowed, and Olivia thought she might have overplayed her hand. She'd already asked about the streaming and got told the media room equipment wasn't compatible with a Wi-Fi signal. Was this 2010?

"Why are you a whiny child?"

"Where is your husband?" Olivia shot back.

The moment the words were out, Olivia wanted to pull them back. A feeling that was only made worse by the narrowing of the woman's eyes.

"I'd suggest you keep your mouth shut and your thoughts to yourself."

It surprised Olivia that Jane didn't just look mean, she actually looked a bit unhinged. There was something not right behind her cold eyes. Eyes that matched the dark smile on her face when she pulled Olivia's phone out of her pocket and held it up in a taunting motion.

It dawned on her a split second before it happened that Jane's intention was to ruin her phone.

Olivia tried to snatch it back, but the hateful woman moved back out of her reach. "My house, my rules."

A low-level panic settled in that was rapidly morphing out of control. If she didn't have her phone, she didn't have her hot spot out of range of the Wi-Fi.

Which meant she couldn't call Nic on her VoIP when she got to safety.

"That's my phone."

"You can have it back tomorrow."

"I want it now."

"Too bad."

Before Olivia could do anything, Jane stared down at the phone in her hand and threw it on the ground, stomping it with the heel of her cowboy boot. Without another glance, she turned on that same heel and left the kitchen.

Raw panic ate at her all the way out of the kitchen and back up to her room, hot tears threatening the whole way.

It was only when she slammed the door that she realized she still held the restaurant magnet in her grip.

Opening her fist, she read the name of the restaurant: Ted's Pizzeria.

And underneath it in tiny letters were the words that could make all the difference.

SUNBURST, MONTANA.

She knew where she was.

Now she just had to figure out how to get that information to Nic.

Trace stared down at all Garner had managed to procure in the past twelve hours and marveled at his baby brother's skills. He knew the man was a badass—nearly two decades as a SEAL had ensured it—but he was tactical as hell.

And his ability to piece together disparate information that actually fit together was nearly otherworldly.

It reminded Trace that, of the two of them, he'd always been the big-picture guy. He made the connections between implications and outcomes. He could calculate possible and probable end results, spinning out scenario after scenario in his mind. That skill had done him well, preparing him for any eventuality and giving him the needed mental bandwidth to pivot if the inputs changed.

Garner's skills were more grounded and focused, his array of maps and satellite imagery—all publicly available—an absolute marvel.

Add on Jake's tactical abilities and Nic's exceptional knowledge of the case and the agency itself, and the four of them made a formidable team.

"I want to run something by all of you," Trace said at last.

When everyone settled, fortified by the food he and Nic had bought earlier, Trace laid it out.

"First, Olivia is the priority. However she was initially identified as the pawn in this, our latest intel suggests the danger around her has likely ratcheted up."

"Walk me through that," Jake probed, reaching for his water. "Hasn't she always been in danger?"

Trace spun out one of those probabilities for them. "With her family, she likely wasn't in physical danger. Yes, being near the misdeeds of the uncle and the vapid lifestyle of the mother is a problem, but we can assume they care for her and love her and aren't looking to harm her."

Garner snorted at that. "The association with them is enough to do that."

It was Nic who stepped in. "Trace is right, though. Her family cares for her. Has her in the best schools. They even tolerate her precocious technical skills. She's loved, albeit ignored or underestimated much of the time. But she wasn't in physical danger in New Jersey."

"So what's changed in your scenario?" Garner asked.

"The uncle's business associates. If someone in the agency is after me..." Trace's gaze drifted to Nic, but he no longer saw resistance to the idea "...we have to figure this case was the one he identified as the pathway to lure me in."

"How many people knew you two were a hot item?" Jake asked, reaching for a handful of chips.

The question was fair, and Trace had to admit, one he should have considered a lot sooner.

"Management knew."

Nic's eyes widened, their discussion on the day she arrived that their team likely knew about their relationship obviously rushing back to her, but she just nodded slightly. "They know everything else. It's safe to assume they knew that, too."

"They don't know everything, but they do know how to use operatives who work well together. Add in a bit of romance, and we become catnip to them in a partner scenario."

"How do you figure that one?" She took a sip of the coffee she preferred over water. "We're a liability."

"Not while we're together. Together we're even more incentivized to keep the other safe."

"Or romantically go down with the ship," Garner added.

Nic's quick "what?" and puzzled face must have matched Trace's as they both swung toward his brother.

"What does that mean?" Trace asked.

"You're operatives. To your point, you're incentivized to keep each other safe. You're also going to be more keen to protect one another. No squealing secrets if the other is captured for fear of putting them in danger."

"That's good." Nic nodded. "It's very good. And it explains some of the grunt duty I got after Trace left."

"Grunt duty?"

"Oh yeah. I wasn't totally persona non grata, and I

pushed for new assignments pretty quick once I realized what was going on, but I got a bit of scut. A few protection details in Europe that were ridiculous in the extreme. A wild-goose chase in the Middle East that had me looking for old security files that had long since been destroyed. And an investigation of a new communications satellite in India that was so on the up-and-up clergy could have written the code."

Jake held up a hand. "How long did this happen?"

"About five or six months."

"For five months after Trace left," Jake pushed, "how often did they keep you out of the office?"

"Every week. I finished one job and moved right into the next. In that stretch I think I slept in my own bed three nights."

"That wasn't scut." Jake shook his head. "That was housecleaning. They got you out so they could reassess what you knew and how dangerous you were from Trace's influence."

"Oh, come on…" Nic broke off, and Trace would bet anything that forgotten conversations had begun spinning in her head. Her voice was quiet when she finally spoke. "I was played."

"Not the right answer," Jake shot back. He wasn't unkind, but there was something unyielding in his tone that snapped Nic to attention.

"What else could it be? There I was, buried in my own head and missing Trace, and I just went along with it."

"They used that all against you. If you weren't a possible threat to them, they'd never have tried any of it," Jake persisted, his attention laser-focused on her. "You're good, and you're passionate about what you do. They had to be sure you weren't going to follow Trace's rogue attitude and employ it in your work going forward."

"But they used me. They're still using me." She looked up, her gaze meeting Trace's, and he saw a world of understanding layered with raw pain. "You're right. About everything. It was you they wanted all along."

Nic stared at the computer screen and filtered through her notes files from the past two years. She knew her own style—matter-of-fact layered over observation—and read and reread her own impressions, memories of each of the jobs coming back to her.

Every word was written with serious dedication to the work and the belief she had in what she was doing. Even those boring jobs—protecting a low-level government flunky in Milan and searching for any anomalies in the satellite plans—had been handled with thorough professionalism.

She'd accept nothing less from herself.

Trace had settled in the bedroom to watch TV, giving her a bit of space. Updates on the Sonics dominating play kept echoing back through the open door.

He hadn't said much to her after Jake's masterful ability to drag her down memory lane and come out with a completely different understanding of what she'd experienced. Instead, all three men seemed to sense that she needed a bit of room to process her thoughts and had agreed to regroup in the morning to finalize plans to get Olivia.

They'd all agreed the child was the focus, and everything else could come after. Taking down Richie Brigante and whatever rogue agent was masterminding the situation took a distant second to Olivia's safety.

"You okay?"

It was only as Trace's words found her that she realized the TV was no longer blaring sports updates. She turned to find him in the entryway of the bedroom.

"I'll take the hide-a-bed out here, and you can have the bed. It's probably a good idea to turn in."

She glanced at the time stamp on her computer and realized just how much time she'd spent lost in her own head. "Sure. Of course." Nic closed her laptop and vowed to put it away for the night. They were meeting early, and she needed the sleep, too.

"How's your head?" She'd watched him throughout the day. He hadn't exhibited the aftereffects of a concussion, so she'd taken that as a lucky outcome. There could have been a far different ending if his attacker had gotten a slightly different angle from behind.

His grin was a bit lopsided. "Fortunately quite hard and stubborn. I've managed to get it down to two aspirin, and I even went six hours since my last dose." That smile fell, replaced with a more serious demeanor. "I'm trying to figure out how we fell right back into old habits earlier. I'm sorry for it, but I've also spent the last few hours trying to figure out the why of it. I don't want to be in that place with you, Nic. For whatever time I have left with you, I'd like it to be positive. I don't want to fight with you."

While it shouldn't have been a surprise, it was an unintended gut punch to hear him mention their time left.

But of course.

It wasn't like she was staying here. Nor were they back together. A few kisses weren't rekindling a relationship, and nothing changed the fact that she had a home and a job to go back to once they found Olivia and got to the bottom of what was going on.

End of story.

So why did it make her so sad to think about leaving?

"No, I don't want to be in that place, either. I want—" The words died in her throat as the reality of what she *did* want simply took over.

She wanted Trace.

Not because their time was limited, though she could admit that was a factor.

And not because they were risking a lot to save Olivia, though that was a factor, too.

But this was so much more.

She wanted him because she'd never stopped wanting him. Not one single second of a single day since they'd been apart.

"What do you want, Nic?"

Trace hadn't moved from his position in the doorway, but he'd gone very still, his neck corded with lines as if he was straining every muscle in his body in order to remain that unmoving.

Time seemed to pause in the space between them as the unspoken promise of what they could have arced between them.

And then she didn't want to wait any longer. Didn't want to argue herself out of it or tempt herself into it. What she wanted didn't sit on either side of that equation.

Oh no, it was so much more.

She wanted the absolute belonging she felt when she was in his arms.

She wanted the heat. The physical union. The endless pleasure. All of it wrapped up in that glorious intimacy she'd never felt with anyone else.

Nic crossed the room, her steps deliberate, until she reached him. Without hesitation or question, she moved into him, wrapping her arms around his neck and gently pulling his head down for a kiss.

Trace hesitated for the briefest of moments. A fraction of a second, really, yet she felt it.

"Is this okay?"

"Oh yeah." He nodded, and she could feel his smile against her lips as he murmured the words. "It's okay in every way."

And then she gave in to all of it.

Trace wrapped his arms tight around her and savored the feel of having Nic pressed against him. Oh how he'd missed her.

It wasn't just the physical—it could never be just the physical—but that had been a part of it all. The sheer want and desire he held for her, every day since they'd met, was a living thing inside of him.

Even when they'd been together, he'd never found a point where they'd had enough of one another. Or had fully sated the most elemental desire between them.

But wow, had they tried.

In the time since, he'd dreamed of her, spent sleepless nights because of her and woken up wanting her. And as he walked them backward into the bedroom, he was determined to make up for the misery of every one of those very long years.

He had the heavy sweatshirt she wore up and over her head, the thin T-shirt she had on under it quickly following. His own clothes came off just as quickly, her hands as impatient as his. Their jeans came next, and she had the advantage over him when she simply reached inside and took him in hand, not even waiting until they were fully naked.

Desire had claws, quickly filling him and taking over. No matter how he'd imagined this—and how slow he'd sworn he would take things—the need between them burned far too hot to wait.

Trace matched her movements, slipping his fingers beneath the elastic of her panties, and was rewarded with a sharp cry of pleasure as her inner muscles clenched around his fingers. She was wet with her pleasure, and he used it ruthlessly to take her up, over, setting a pace that she more than kept up with.

They pushed each other on, a delicious battle of touch and taste, of want and long-denied hunger. Somewhere along the way, they lost the rest of their clothing, falling onto the bed pressed to each other.

And long, endless kisses later, as he rose up over her and slid into that welcoming warmth, Trace was forced to admit the truth. Home had always been the most elusive of places for him.

But Nicola Miles was his home.

He'd known it on a soul-deep level from the first.

And he knew with everything he was that she would be forever.

Chapter 16

Nic lay wrapped up in Trace and gave herself a moment to simply enjoy. To ignore the endlessly circling thoughts that always filled her mind. And to just be in the moment. Present and perfectly sated as the heavy weight of his body kept her warm.

The wind howled outside the windows, the promised storm doing its work.

"What time is it?" Trace's voice was heavy with sleep as he turned his head to look at the bedside clock. "Three thirty. That wind is something else out there."

Despite her best efforts to be in the moment and enjoy what she'd wanted for so long, reality crashed back in. "We're going to have to find her in what's left behind after that storm's blown itself out."

His hold tightened around her. "We will find her, Nic. I promise you that."

"It's what else we're going to find that worries me. People know we're here, Trace. The truck is proof of that. How they know, I have no idea, but they know, and we're going to have to plan for that now. Our ability to sneak onto the property has likely vanished."

They'd tossed around a few theories with Jake and Garner earlier, but the fact that they were detected in town so quickly was a concern. It suggested that someone expected they would be found here and on some level had shared their identities in advance.

But who'd seen them?

She supposed the employees of the hotel could be in on it, but Trace had checked them in while she stayed in the truck, and they'd kept a low profile overall.

"Jake had a few theories on that. Because he's the newest one of the group, he was going to spend some time in the lobby bar. See if he could get anyone talking or if he overheard any of the staff talking."

"I get the sense he can be rather persuasive."

Nic took definite solace knowing Jake was looking into things. And it also reinforced Trace's point yesterday. He and his partners were all in on this. It was incredibly reassuring to know she and Trace weren't facing this alone.

If she were even more honest, it was the first time since Trace left the agency that she felt like someone truly had her back. Which should have been an even bigger sign she'd stayed in DC too long.

But what was the alternative?

Wyoming.

With Trace.

Supporting the private work he and Garner and now Jake are doing.

"I know what we're facing, Nic." Trace settled a finger beneath her chin, gently lifting her head so their gazes met. "I know the danger, and I'm prepared for it. But I don't want to give any more of these moments up. I have you until daylight, and I can't see my way to being sorry for that."

"I know." She lifted her lips to his, pushing all that was to come outside of the bed.

They were committed to seeing this job through and getting Olivia back safely. That couldn't happen tonight, nor could it happen in the middle of a snowstorm. So they'd take the time until daylight. Especially with the knowledge it might be all they would get.

Nic was already up and out of bed when he woke up again. They'd made love twice more before dawn, and he let the sheer joy of that move through him as he showered and got ready for the day.

It was a gap in time—a few hours for just them—and now it was over. He needed to bury the emotions that came from being with her again and get his head firmly in place.

In less than forty-eight hours, his home had been breached, and he'd been targeted within an hour of arriving in a small Montana border town.

He was the target.

And unlike every op he'd run before, he had no intel to support the work they were doing. It was all theories and scenarios, with nothing concrete or certain.

Except the location. Every instinct he had told him the property they'd narrowed in on was the right one.

"Trace!"

He nearly collided with Nic as he headed into the suite's living room, excitement riding high on her face. "The texting program. On Eloisa's phone. Did she bite?"

With all that had happened the day before, he'd forgotten about checking the program last night. "She hadn't all day yesterday, but I forgot to look last night." He pulled his phone out of his pocket, vaguely remembering a notification ding that he hadn't answered.

"Hot damn."

The words escaped him on a hard exhale as he reviewed the program he'd set up. Not only had Eloisa taken the bait, but he had full access to everything she'd done on her phone since five o'clock the day before.

"I'm in."

Nic hovered near his elbow, and Trace kept the phone turned her way as he scrolled. His program didn't capture the names of her contacts, but they could reverse look up the numbers. In the meantime, he could gather context from several. "Looks like text messages with her brother. What looks like her lover on this one."

"There's her text back to the boutique." Nic leaned closer, her voice growing puzzled. "And another string of texts on a different number. Purring about her lover's anatomy, among other things. Those are some graphic compliments," she added.

"Puffery at its finest."

She glanced up at him. "What do you mean? It looks like she's keeping two fish on the hook."

"She's keeping the rich fish on the hook." Trace reread the last few messages. "But read them. The sex talk to the fish is over the top. Especially when you look at the other one. It's sexier and way more subtle."

He handed Nic his phone so that he could get his computer and look at the texting program there. In a matter of minutes, he had the two text strings pulled up side by side onscreen. He set his laptop on the kitchen counter so they could both look at the variance in the messages.

"See there," he said. "Look at the cadence and the tone. It drips with fake praise."

"I see your point. Especially knowing his age and life stage."

"She's his prize, and she's going to make sure she stays that way."

"There's something else there. Look." Nic pointed at one of the last messages to the man who seemed to be her actual paramour. "She's mentioning how she can't wait to see him. She's supposed to be in New York with the old beau. But here she's looking to get with the other guy."

"It's a sign. And—" He stopped, registering the number of the boyfriend she probably actually wanted. "That's a 571 area code."

"I have a 571 area code."

"So do I."

"What's Eloisa doing sending seductive messages to a Northern Virginia area code?"

"I could give you two guesses," Trace said, "but you're probably only going to need one."

Garner and Jake arrived shortly after they made the discoveries on Eloisa's phone, and Nic got them up to speed while Trace looked through whatever other data he could get off of Eloisa's phone.

The text messages were the most informative, until he hit the mother lode with her last mobile credit card transactions.

"She's in Montana."

"Olivia's mother?" Nic looked up from where she was studying maps with Garner.

"She flew in yesterday morning and made mobile payments at LaGuardia and Chicago O'Hare before flying into Bozeman. She had one more transaction there, which was food."

"Layover to a smaller plane?" Garner asked.

"Maybe, maybe not," Trace said. "It's a four-hour drive so someone could have picked her up. But she made a purchase, so we've verified location."

"Any texts with Olivia?" Nic asked. "When I scanned the details before, I didn't see anything but wanted to check. She's got a 973 area code."

Now that Nic flagged it, there *were* a lack of texts with her own child. It was only as he moved down through the list that he saw the sad reality of Eloisa's parenting.

Her last text to Olivia was three days ago.

"I found it. She sent a note three days ago telling Olivia to be good for Uncle Richie and a smiley face blowing a kiss."

"Three days?" Nic asked. "She's had plenty of time for sexy texts but can't be bothered to check in on her child?"

"Mother of the year," Trace muttered, well aware of the judgment that dripped from his tone. With his own mother's actions so recently churned up in his thoughts, he understood how easy it would be to equate the two women.

Only those feelings of abandonment and inadequacy didn't come.

And with that realization—that he could be angry for Olivia and not channel it into his own pain—Trace recognized the victory.

Instead, all he felt was sheer anger for a child who deserved so much better. From all the adults around her, yes, but from her mother most of all.

"So we need to plan for the mother, too." Garner turned to Nic. "We'll play this how you want, but if we snatch the kid out of her family's hands with no clear evidence she's been harmed, we're risking kidnapping charges."

"Child endangerment," Trace snapped, unwilling to get into the gray areas of what they were going to do. "We have every reason to believe the child's life is at risk, either directly or indirectly via the people her uncle has aligned himself with."

"Your sheriff's support would go a long way toward reinforcing that as well," Nic said, obviously undeterred on their course of action.

"I'm not saying we don't do it," Garner added. "I don't want Olivia sent back to those people."

Trace didn't want that, either. Those nonexistent text messages checking in on her only reinforced it.

Jake had been fairly quiet up to now, adding in a few tactical thoughts but giving them room to plot and plan.

But his assessments from the start had been spot-on, and Trace admired the man's ability to listen and work toward a solution.

"That doesn't change the fact that the mother is another layer in this we have to plan for. And since it is her child," Jake added, "we can assume she'll either be a loose cannon or will use the situation to act like one."

Despite repeated admonitions to trust her instincts, Nic found little to feel good about as she prepared to head out with the men. Jake and Hogan had already gone out and inspected Garner's SUV, finding nothing of concern. The two feet of snow they'd gotten overnight had likely helped as a deterrent, but it created new problems this morning.

Namely, how were they going to navigate a major op in the biting cold and wintry landscape? And also, how were they going to avoid detection wearing full gear as they traipsed through fields of blinding white?

Garner was packing up the additional firepower he and Jake had brought along. After that, he planned to go out and join man and dog to dig out the SUV, and then they'd reassess from there.

Nic and Trace had been left to finalize their entry point into the property and then determine how they were going to navigate the snow-covered terrain.

"It's a blinding white nightmare," she muttered as she once again considered their options. They'd narrowed it down to what looked like a work road in the back of the property or an entrance on the west side of the acreage that sloped downhill and wasn't easily visible from someone standing on higher ground.

Either option still put them at least a half mile from the house, tromping through a landscape that would slow them down.

Should they wait?

Each time she asked herself the question, she quickly dismissed it. Olivia might not have the time, and that made it an unacceptable option.

But getting her out in these conditions was damn near impossible.

"I heard you muttering all the way out in the living room," Trace said.

"Did you get the pack made?"

Trace nodded in the direction of the living area. "Food and water as well as blankets and a few more layers of clothing. If we need to snatch Olivia, we can't assume she'll be in winter attire."

They couldn't, and it had been his advance thinking that had ensured there was a pack at all. One more sign Nic was swirling in various scenarios that refused to settle in her mind.

"At this point we should just walk up to the damn front door." She tossed her phone on top of the small pile she'd built on the bed, the frustration mounting.

"We could."

"We most certainly cannot."

Trace quickly warmed to the idea. "Yeah, actually, we can."

"They're expecting us. Showing up at the front door isn't exactly a surprise attack."

"Right, *us*. But Garner and Jake showing up at the front door, us hidden in the back of the SUV, is not what they're expecting."

It wasn't just his excitement, Nic admitted to herself. His point had merit. Brigante and whoever he was working with would be on high alert for any intruders, but they were expecting her and Trace.

"With what excuse?"

"Jake's got the dog. We say they're tracking a missing elderly man who is presumed lost in the storm. Could they come onto the property to look?"

"A house full of criminals isn't going to see through that?"

"That's the beauty of it. It's so obvious, why would they question it? And all we need is to get close enough to go find Olivia. You and I slip out the back while they're creating the distraction at the door."

The idea skated that strange borderline of nearly brilliant coupled with practically insane.

Which made it so enticing.

"All we need is Olivia, Nic. The rest of this can wait. The only goal is to get her out of there."

That had been her only goal, but as they'd learned more over the past forty-eight hours, it had shifted. Expanded. Because now it was about keeping Trace safe, too.

"One thing at a time, Nic." He reached out and pulled her close, and she went willingly into his arms.

They hadn't spoken today about what happened last

night. A part of her wondered if she should feel strange about that, but the bigger part of her had simply gone about her day, secure in the knowledge she'd made the right choice.

The only choice.

There was a future that yawned in front of them, one that had always looked like it would be spent apart. A night making love wasn't going to change that.

But at least she got the night.

And more than that, she'd gotten a chance to address and maybe repair what had torn them apart. It didn't mean they were getting a happily-ever-after—was that a real thing?—but it had given her an opportunity to perhaps erase some of the destruction that had been left in their wake two years ago.

It was a gift, she realized as she lifted her head from his chest and looked up at him. Their old lives and old relationship were gone, but they no longer needed to be painful memories.

In a dreamy sort of slow motion that belied the urgency of what was happening around them, their lips met, sweet and trusting and full of that banked passion she'd always associated with him.

There was no *easy* with Trace Withrow. No smooth, frictionless ride. No part of his personality that didn't demand everything from his partner.

It was no less than he demanded from himself.

The night before had been amazing. A chance to steal back some of what the past two years had taken from both of them. But this? Now? It was the quiet acknowledgment that they could still comfort each other, even after all this time.

Her fingertips explored the broad planes of his back,

drifting over the firm, lean muscle there. His hands spanned the length of her spine, holding her close and pressing their bodies together, keeping them connected.

So much waited outside the door, and they would face all of it.

But for these last few lingering moments, Nic wanted to take the time for herself.

For them.

And for all they'd never have again.

The snowfall was as bad as expected, Trace acknowledged as Garner drove slowly out of the hotel parking lot. He'd brought chains for the tires, and they'd put them on as the last step before leaving the hotel. The measure would offer significantly more protection for the drive, but it was going to sorely limit their speed. One more thing they'd discussed and turned over, going through the tactical considerations for and against.

It was Nic who'd suggested they could use the chains as an element in their story, talking about how bad the roads were, yet how desperate they were to find their fictitious missing elderly man.

Garner and Jake were game for the ruse and had already worked out their cover and the patter they'd employ between them.

It was a good plan.

He and Nic had made a hiding spot in the far back of the SUV and had agreed to at least ride there, even if they hadn't covered themselves in the reams of items. They figured they could risk comms devices based on the ruse of the search, and he could hear Garner and Jake as they worked through a few tactical points.

Nic had Trace's laptop open and was reading through

Eloisa's texts again as well as what had come in overnight. More over-the-top sexy texts with the boyfriend back in New York. And nothing with the other one.

"Anything new?"

"Beyond the nauseating sex talk?" Nic gave a mock shiver. "I will never be able to scrub that out of my brain."

"But still nothing with the other one?"

"Not a thing. They're together," Nic said, excited. "Can you track GPS on the phone?"

"I can triangulate off the last text."

Nic handed over the computer. "Beware your eyes don't burn."

He grinned at her. "I never took you for a prude." Since he knew for a fact that she most certainly wasn't, it was fun to tease her.

"Those are pornographic."

"Way to tease a guy," Jake said through their comms. "You can't read me a few?"

It was enough to break the tension that had risen with each slow mile, a reminder of what it was like to work in a team. Sure, it was gallows humor, but how many missions had Trace been on through the years that carried that lighthearted teasing as a bonding method? Wasn't that part of why he and Garner worked so well?

The intimacy of the work—the familiarity and rapport that was one person knowing another, trusting another— was fundamentally essential to the outcome.

It played through his mind as Trace went to work capturing the GPS coordinates.

Eloisa was the wild card in the mix they hadn't been able to plan for. They could only assume she was somehow a part of things and present at the ranch. But if she was the side piece, hanging out somewhere else, it split the focus of their quarry, potentially in their favor.

The snow was slowing their movements, but it would slow everyone else's, too.

And if Eloisa wasn't there, that meant someone in Brigante's orbit wasn't, either.

"The mother's the connector."

"To what?" Nic asked.

"All of it. Think about it. She knows the brother's business. She knows how smart the kid is. All the vapid behavior and running with the boyfriends? It gets her out of the way and makes her look innocent."

"But she isn't." Nic shook her head. "She's been the outlier from the start. And there hasn't been a damn thing we can pin on her."

"Queen bee who won't get her hands dirty." Garner's voice boomed through the comms. "But she's running the whole thing."

"How could we have missed it?" Nic pressed, spiky frustration in her voice. "If she's this close and running the whole damn thing, why is nothing implicating her? At all?"

"Because her number one drone is in your organization. She's got him doing her dirty work for her. Which likely means missing or doctored files and a whole lot of 'look over here' distraction."

As he tried on Garner's assessment, Trace had to admit it fit. Even if he gave his old workplace the benefit of the doubt, the volume of work was overwhelming. A well-respected operative could work with that, doing his dirty work in small batches over a long period of time so as not to get caught.

Patient, just waiting to strike.

Wasn't that the message in the challenge coins?

I've been here all along.

"You got those coordinates?" Jake asked.

Trace tapped a few last keys, and the coordinates popped up. He read them off, knowing Jake was mapping to the coordinates of the ranch.

"Damn it." Jake added a few more inventive curses full of excitement. "The latitude and longitude's a match for the ranch."

"She's pinging off the same cell tower," Nic said. "But that doesn't mean she's in the house. The property's large, and there hasn't been a single text between Eloisa and her brother or to her daughter that she's arrived in Montana."

Again, Trace thought, there was that proof point that stuck a hard landing: no communication with her child. It didn't necessarily mean everything, but it meant something. He'd stake his life on it. What bothered him was the fact that he was staking everyone else's on it, too.

Everyone, he realized as he heard the chatter in his ear as Nic, Garner and Jake talked through it all, that mattered.

Chapter 17

With coats, blankets and several backpacks layered over top of them, Nic lay nestled beside Trace in the back of the SUV. In any other circumstance, it might have bordered on cozy—minus the sharp metal handle of who-knew-what that poked her back.

But that sharp tool was just the discomfort she needed to keep her head in the game. They had more intel now that Trace had access to Eloisa's phone, but they were still flying blind on so much.

Who was the operative from the agency involved in all this?

What were they running here in the far north?

And who was the mercenary who'd gotten killed in the midst of it all?

"Push it aside," Trace whispered in her ear.

She turned to him, his features shadowed under the thick cover. "We don't know what we're facing."

"We're getting Olivia. That's the only goal here. The rest can and will come later."

"It might not be that easy."

"Maybe not, but we'll deal with that if it comes. We've got the element of surprise on our side. We've got firepower. And we've got a really mean-looking dog."

"I heard that," Jake said in their ears.

"Hogan's beautiful," Nic rushed to add. "But he's got a serious intimidation factor."

"That's why I love my boy," Jake cooed, obviously sweet-talking to Hogan, who'd patiently waited in one of the passenger bucket seats behind Garner.

Nic left him to the pre-op pep talk. Which, like the blanket overlay in the back, would have been cute and funny if the stakes weren't so high.

"Pulling into the driveway," Garner said, detailing everything he saw as he drove slowly. Nic pictured each place he described, matching it to the aerial photos they'd reviewed of the property.

"Outbuilding is just where we think it is," Jake added. The old decrepit stables they'd read about on the property's real estate listing were the closest to the house. "Should be condemned," he added, "but it's got a roof, so it'll work in our favor."

They'd aligned on specific hiding places if Nic and Trace felt they needed one with Olivia, and the stables had topped the list. The short distance from the house would work in their favor as they spirited her away, and the likely hiding places inside from stalls to tack room to a hayloft added to the building's potential.

Trace's hand closed over Nic's as the SUV came to a stop. "We're getting her out of there."

She squeezed back and closed her eyes. They'd prepared, and all four of them, as well as the dog, were trained with the highest degree of skill.

They had to be flawless on this, and she knew they would be.

Because anything else could get a child killed.

* * *

Trace kept checking his watch. Garner and Jake had been out of the SUV for more than four minutes, and so far no one had come to the door. They'd kept up congenial conversation, talking about the search for anyone who might be listening, playing their roles as search-and-rescue to perfection.

"No one's answering," Garner drawled. "Maybe you and Hogan start the search, and I'll see if I can find anyone and let 'em know why we're here."

"Man's been missing for a few hours. I'm not hopeful on this one."

"Talk like that's not gonna help." Garner pushed some heat into his words. "He's depending on us."

"Yes, sir."

Trace pictured the slightly cheeky expression that likely matched the words before he heard Jake give Hogan a few commands, the sound of them walking echoing through his earpiece.

"Hello! Anyone home!" Garner pounded on the door once more, hollering as he did. "Hell—"

His words ended abruptly as a new voice floated through the comms. "What do you want?"

The female voice was low and smoky, and Trace turned to face Nic. "Eloisa?"

"Not her," Nic whispered. "Voice is too low and not accented."

Garner kept up his congenial tone, one he knew his brother could project in spades. He was a big man who knew how to disarm people with big personality charm, and that was pumping full-bore through their earpieces. "I'm sorry to bother you. I'm local search-and-rescue.

We've got an elderly man missing. He's got dementia, and his family's panicked he got lost."

The woman didn't sound convinced. "Out here? I'm sure he couldn't be on our property. We're rather remote."

"They broke down about a mile up the road. While the husband and wife were working on getting the truck back up and running, the old man took off."

"That's hardly my problem."

"My partner and I will stay out of your way. Just wanted you to know we're here."

The comment was easygoing but punctuated with the underlying point that she didn't really have a choice in the matter.

"Well, I'll need to see if my husband is okay with this."

"Sure. We'll get started. Have him come on out." As if an afterthought, he added, "Name's Garner, ma'am. Garner Pinnip."

"Cheeky bastard," Trace muttered, his brother's joke not lost on him. When Nic just looked at him askance, he smiled. "Garner's long-standing joke. The scientific name of seals are pinnipeds."

"It's an oldie but goodie," Garner said under his breath. "She's flustered but didn't kick me out. Let's figure the husband'll come out and make a fuss, and then you two can get to work."

Time moved like a drip-feed, but Trace and Nic waited it out. Nothing suggested there was anyone else around beyond the purported husband, and Jake kept a steady relay of information from his side as he and Hogan moved over the property.

Garner did the same routine with the man who came to the door. Although Nic added color commentary identifying the man as Richie Brigante based on his voice, all Jake and Garner got from him was the fake name John Smith.

"So they're keeping that routine up," Trace said.

"Olivia said the other man was John," Nic hissed.

"More to suggest that he's the one who was killed at my front door."

"Our front door," Garner corrected as he'd obviously moved out of the front door's line of sight. "You're clear. I'm coming around the back to get my gear. Duck out when I do."

Garner made a big show of hollering instructions to Jake, who was some distance away, not even looking in the back seat. Nic scrambled out first, and Trace followed, staying low behind the body of the SUV.

Garner slammed the back door closed while Trace and Nic remained low and out of sight. Jake kept watch at a distance, giving instructions as he kept an eye on the house.

"Couple's still in the windows, looking out at us. Stay behind the SUV until I give the signal."

Trace and Nic remained low, but he knew she was as desperate to move as he was.

"Stay the course," Garner's voice echoed in their earpieces. "Wife left the windows. Brigante can't be far behind. He might not stay gone, but it'll give you a chance to get up against the house."

"What if Olivia's not even in there?" Despite her whisper, Nic's question was as powerful as a gunshot.

"Then we find a new plan," Trace asserted.

"Jake and Garner are out in the open. We're at risk of discovery. I've put you all at risk."

He heard the increasing notes of panic and turned to face her. "We will find her. Here or wherever these people have taken her. We've done the work and made our plans. Now's the time to see them through."

"They're gone." Garner's voice filled both their ears. "Make a run for it."

Trace took another few beats, his gaze holding hers. "We're getting her out of here. Believe me when I say that."

Nic nodded. "I believe you."

"Then let's go."

Nic followed Trace, moving for the spot on the outer wall of the house they'd identified as their goal. It got them out of view from the main windows and a chance to regroup.

There wasn't any sign of Olivia, but it wasn't like they were going to advertise the presence of the kid, either. And even if she was perfectly fine, it wasn't a stretch to think she wasn't going to be outside the morning after a blizzard.

Although heavy, the snow had a powdery consistency that was easier to navigate than a thicker wet dumping, and they crossed the space between the SUV and the house quickly.

Trace looked at the distance they'd run and shook his head. "I don't like the tracks in the snow."

"Hogan and I will come back that way," Jake offered, already circling back toward the driveway. "We'll make it look good if they're watching and get something else out of the back seat. I'll have Hogan mess up the footprints a bit."

Satisfied they'd done as much as they could to avoid detection, Nic kept on, Trace behind her.

She stared up at the house, assessing where Olivia might be. The living room was at the front of the house, and some instinct had her moving opposite of that. Would they have wanted her near them or would they put her in a room farther out of range of whatever they might be discussing and planning?

"I think we should start at the back," Nic suggested. "They'd either want to deliberately keep her out of earshot, or she'd pull a teenager move and take the back of the house anyway. Either way, I think we start there."

"Let's do it."

The house was large, two stories tall and far more modern than the rest of the property. Nic mentally pulled up the real estate images and remembered the large bedroom at the back of the second floor. Picking up the pace, she stilled at the corner before slowly edging her head around the back of the house.

The yard was empty, the ground still pristine and untouched from the snowfall.

"We need something to throw at the windows." Nic reached down and tried to pack some snow in her gloves, but the light, fluffy consistency floated through her fingers.

"We can use some of the nuts from the trail mix we packed." Trace dug a single serving out of his backpack and ripped it open, dumping some nuts into her palm. "Give it a try."

She tossed a handful up toward the windows, lightly grazing the glass but doubtful she'd made enough noise to attract attention. "You try it."

Trace already had his gloves off and tossed a few more nuts at the window, a light ping echoing down.

"Olivia." Nic used a heavy whisper as she tossed another handful up. "Olivia!"

The window flew up suddenly, before a head peeked out. "Nic!"

"Shhh." Nic lifted a finger to her lips, relief flooding through her at the confirmation Olivia was safe. Now they needed to get her out. "Can you get out of the house? I just need you to get to a door."

"I don't have a coat or my phone."

"We've got a coat for you. Shoes, too."

"Can I toss down my computer?"

It was Trace who spoke up beside Nic. "Send down whatever you need to, honey. We'll keep it safe."

Olivia ducked back in the room, and Nic turned to face him. "That's sweet, but we need to go."

"She needs to feel some measure of control. And she needs that laptop. And you can't afford to miss out on whatever's on it."

Before Nic could press him, Trace held up a hand. "I deliberately kept that as a distant third because it *is* a distant third. But you don't want these people getting their hands on it, either. Two birds, Nic."

Olivia's head reappeared along with a pillowcase in her hand. She leaned over as far as she could, the pillowcase still ten feet above them.

"Drop it," Trace ordered. He easily caught the machine before dragging his pack off and stuffing it inside.

"I'll meet you out front," Olivia promised before ducking back in the house.

"Let's get out of here." Trace extended a hand and Nic took it. "We're getting her home."

"I wouldn't be so sure about that."

The voice was eerily familiar, but it wasn't until Nic and Trace turned that she had the confirmation.

Because the man about ten yards away? The one with

the gun at the end of his arms pointed directly at them? He was her boss.

Dirk Rannell.

"What are you doing here?" Nic blurted.

The gun never wavered as Dirk looked first at her, then at Trace and then back to her again. "What I've been aiming to do for the last three years. Getting rid of both of you."

Dirk Rannell was the operative who wanted to take him down?

Trace kept going over and over that truth and couldn't reconcile the deeds of the past few days with the man he knew. Or had known.

Dirk Rannell had been on every list of teammates he and Nic had gone through over the challenge coins, and they'd each dismissed him without thinking, never once considering him capable of not only going rogue but creating such a nefarious mess.

"Dirk," Trace said at last. "What is this possibly about?"

"Haven't you figured it out, Withrow? It's all been about getting to you. I knew she'd run straight to you the moment things got tough. And it was easy to see just how attached she was getting to the kid. It practically dripped from every report she wrote."

"Why would I ever figure this?" Trace edged in front of Nic, putting her out of immediate firing range. He sensed her frustration but refused to let her take any more risks on his behalf. "You're one of the most respected operatives in our office. You and I came up together. We worked together. I trusted you!"

The anger rose along with the litany of their working relationship, and Trace was shocked to realize just how badly it hurt. A knife not just plunged in deep but twisted round and round to cause maximum pain.

"You know the work, Withrow. The job's changed since you and I went in. The good guys have decided to make rules that only favor them. Doesn't matter what the rule of law is. Or international rules of war. Or even the most basic rules of diplomacy. It's all about who's got the best intel and the balls to wield it. Which is why I decided to get my fair share."

Although Trace couldn't find it in him to deny Dirk's points, it was that last comment—the flip over into acceptance and self-dealing—that he refused to accept.

The work had always been the work. Those in charge were going to keep managing the tools in their arsenal to advance their own gains.

That was why Trace got out.

And it was why he believed in the future he was creating here in the northern wilderness with Garner and Jake. He took the jobs. He helped the ones who had no one to stand for them.

Most of all, Trace had channeled that very same anger Dirk carried into something that worked for the benefit of others, not destruction. And then he got to go home and work with his horses and live a life that, while not exactly simple, wasn't about navigating other people's shades of gray.

"Why'd you kill that guy on my property?"

"John was a tool."

"And kidnapping a kid?"

"It's hardly kidnapping for her to spend time with her beloved family. But I have to say, she's an even more useful tool."

"How so?"

Three more people stepped from the side of the house. The man he recognized from photos as Richie Brigante. A woman who stood beside him and hadn't been a part of Nic's intel. And a man wearing a police chief's uniform.

"Her skills have given us all the support and contacts we need here in our little corner of the world."

But it was the fourth person who stepped out that made Trace realize just how badly they'd all been played.

Eloisa Brigante stood head-to-toe in winter gear.

And held her daughter tight in her arms, a gun pressed to the child's head.

"No!" The scream welled in Nic's throat, primal and raw, as she fought to get around Trace.

What was this? And how had she missed so clearly that Dirk Rannell was a lying scumbag piece of crap and Eloisa Brigante was the devil?

She held a gun to her child's head. Her own child. It was the epitome of every bad cop movie Nic had ever seen.

And it hurt. Deep down where she'd buried all the aching grief over her childhood and those years in foster care when she'd have given anything to know why her mother abandoned her.

But now? Based on the gaping maw of pain watching Olivia deal with the same, Nic realized that wound had never truly closed.

She'd simply covered over it with work and training and field ops.

"Give me Olivia," Nic begged. "She's not a part of this."

"Oh but she really is." Eloisa held her daughter more tightly against her. "Her skills and abilities are like a secret weapon. One no one can even see coming."

"I'm sorry, Nic." Tears spilled down Olivia's cheeks, making them raw and red in the cold air. "I'm so sorry you're here. Because of me."

"I'm here to help you." Nic edged her way out from behind Trace's back. "You will never, ever owe me an apology for that."

"Please let them go." Olivia's sobs grew harder, her shoulders shaking in her mother's grip.

"Olivia." Eloisa shook her. "Stop it! Right now!"

The yelling only made the child cry harder, and Nic moved a few steps closer.

Eloisa's hand shook from holding the gun. "Don't move!"

And then it all broke wide-open.

From behind Eloisa and Olivia, Hogan leaped over a snowbank, snarling and feral as he knocked Eloisa down.

Trace moved the moment the commotion began, as dark and feral as the dog as he leaped straight for Rannell.

Jake and Garner followed up with additional rear attacks on Richie and the woman.

Nic trusted they'd all do their work and used the commotion to race to Olivia, dragging the girl to her feet and spiriting her out of the mess.

"I'm so sorry." Olivia continued to sob, but Nic only pulled her closer, half holding her, half supporting her as they ran toward the SUV.

"Stay with me, sweetie. It's okay."

Nic got to the SUV and opened the door, shoving the child inside. "I need you to stay here until I—" She broke off as a wall of field agents came racing toward them.

She recognized a few as fellow operatives from the office. They moved in unison and carried enough firepower for a large army.

And they'd come to help.

It was the last agent, bringing up the rear, who stopped her. Dirk's boss, Abraham Squires.

"Good work, Miles."

"Thank you, sir."

An all clear was hollered from the direction of the house, angry shouts and dog barks echoing along with it.

But it was the gentle smile that lit up Abraham's face that had her taking her first easy breath. "You don't think we'd let you face this one alone, now, did you?"

"Honestly, sir, I thought—"

He nodded, his face instantly going sober. "You did think you were alone on this."

"Well, yes, I did."

"I'm sorry I couldn't tell you. And I'm sorry it took us so long to get here today." He glanced around. "Damn snow."

"It worried us, too."

"Us?" His eyebrows rose. "Withrow's here, too?"

"Yes, sir. Around back."

"I figured as much."

"I know I broke protocol, and I fully own my actions. Please don't hold Trace or Garner Withrow or their friend Jake Stilton accountable for my actions."

"While I appreciate the self-sacrifice, it won't be necessary. Nor am I holding any civilians accountable for ensuring a rogue agent on my team is no longer able to continue his dark deeds." Abraham glanced over to the SUV where Olivia was huddled in one of the back bucket seats. "Now, I think there's someone who needs far more of your time than I do." He patted Nic on the shoulder. "She's far more important than the trash out back. I'll go clean that up for you."

The man walked off, leaving her to Olivia.

Nic closed the SUV door before walking around the back and climbing in the other side, taking the seat next to her. "How are you?"

"Fine."

"How are you really?"

"I'll be fine."

Nic picked up one of the blankets they'd packed for the express purpose of staying warm in the event they got stranded, and covered the child.

For all her bravado since that first time they met, Olivia looked very small as Nic spread the blanket over her.

"You don't have to be fine, you know. Not right now. Or next week. Or even next month. But one of these days, I promise you, you will be."

"My mom—" Olivia broke off on a sob. "My mom tried to hurt me."

"I know she did." Nic shifted out of the seat and wedged herself on the floor of the SUV, kneeling beside Olivia. "She won't hurt you again. She's not going to get the chance."

"She's supposed to love me."

"Yes, she is."

"And she doesn't."

In reality, Nic knew the answer wasn't that simple, but now wasn't the time to try to explain it to Olivia. It would be a journey she'd face for the rest of her life.

But in that moment, as she reached out and took the young girl into her arms in a tight hug, Nic vowed she would be there to help her find the answers.

Always.

Chapter 18

Trace navigated the stream on the south end of the property with Magnum, giving the horse a late-afternoon treat as a reward for the riding they'd done all day across the ranch. Spring was doing its steady march toward summer and now here in early June they were dealing with a scorcher.

Three months.

It had been almost three months since Nic arrived and they'd had their adventure taking down Dirk Rannell and saving Olivia.

Trace had learned a lot since then.

The ways they'd used the child's intelligence to map out an illegal trade route up into Canada.

The hot love affair Dirk had been carrying on with Olivia's mother.

Even the local police chief who'd been bribed into supporting them and who had ultimately made him and Nic at the hotel when they arrived in Montana. It was that same police chief who'd firebombed the truck and damn it if that still didn't chafe.

But he and Garner had already begun work under the hood of a new one, and it was coming along. Jake was settling into ranch life, his patience and skills with the equine program something special.

Jake and Garner had held the fort down when Trace flew to DC for a week to testify in front of an oversight committee. He saw a lot of old colleagues and kissed the asses of several politicians who had questions about the events that went down in Montana. He got those garlic-and-butter mussels he loved at his favorite restaurant in Georgetown. He even spent an aimless afternoon roaming a few of the Smithsonian buildings.

But he hadn't seen Nic.

Nor had she reached out.

He'd heard rumblings that she was up for Rannell's job, and he hoped like hell she got it. He'd like nothing more than to see her get a promotion out of all the crap that had gone down.

So he'd come home to Liar's Gulch and dedicated himself to putting it all in the past.

He knelt down at the stream and cupped his hands, drinking the crisp, fresh water. The snowmelt had been running for weeks on end, and the water had finally lowered enough to actually look like a creek bed again.

All of which would have been just fine for a late spring day that felt like summer if the hairs on the back of his neck hadn't stood up.

Whirling, he was on his feet, his hand reaching for the gun at his back when he came face-to-face with Nic.

She stood about ten feet away, her gun in hand.

"You like pulling a loaded weapon on innocent men drinking from streams?" The words came out as he'd hoped they would—lazy and insolent—even as his heart slammed in his chest at seeing her again.

"Maybe I do."

"What are you doing here?"

"I was looking for someone."

"Find him?"

She smiled at that, even though she never lowered the gun. "Well, I'm trying to decide if Annie Oakley had words of wisdom or if she missed the mark."

"I thought she never missed the mark."

Ignoring the bad pun, she kept on with her thought. "She's the one who claimed, if Hollywood show tunes are to be believed…" Nic moved a few steps closer "…that you can't get a man with a gun. Do you think that's true?"

"I don't particularly love being on the receiving end of one."

She opened the gun to show it was empty before dropping it to her side. "I don't love aiming one, so I guess that makes us even."

"What are you doing here?"

"I came to share my news."

"You got the promotion?" Even with his pounding heartbeat and desperate need to touch her, he couldn't deny how happy he was for her.

"I did."

"That's great. You deserve it."

That crystal gaze never moved off his face. "I turned it down."

"You did?"

"It didn't seem like a good choice. Now that I'm the legal guardian to a teenager."

"You're fostering Olivia?"

"Yep. She's been with me since Montana, but the courts made it official last week."

"That's great, Nic."

And it was. He'd known from the start there was something special about her bond with the child. Olivia had a long road ahead as she worked to accept the failings of her family, and Trace knew Nic would be the ideal person to help her through it.

"It is pretty great. She's an amazing young woman, and I'm just grateful she's willing to follow me."

"To DC?"

Nic took a few steps closer, the empty gun hanging at her side. "We're looking to go a bit farther afield."

"Virginia's got some great places. Great schools, too."

She stepped a few paces closer, dropping the gun at her feet. "Not my style."

"Maryland's good."

And then she closed the gap completely and was so close he could feel the heat of her body. "Olivia and I both agree Wyoming feels more like our style."

That wild ride of adrenaline kept pumping through his body in a rushing stream. "And do what?"

"Well, it seems as if I'm in the market for a job. I hear there might be room on a team-for-hire for someone who's not always willing to play by the rules."

Trace stared at her, hardly able to believe she was here, let alone what she was asking. "You want to live here?"

"Live here. Work here. Play here." She lifted her arms and wrapped them around his neck. "Love here."

"What changed your mind?"

"Nothing changed my mind. Not when I got it set on coming here. Well, really on staying here, since I was already thinking I could make this place home about an hour into my last visit."

"Could have told me."

It was the first hitch he'd seen since laying eyes on her again. A sadness that turned down her lips in a subtle frown. "I should have told you. But my mind was also set on that amazing kid. She needs me, Trace. And I think I need her, too. And I had to make sure this was right for her."

"You're going to be a great mother figure to her."

"She needs a father figure, too."

The unspoken question slammed into him with the force of a bullet, and he staggered back a few paces. "Me?"

"I think we'd make a pretty great family. If you're up for it?"

Not even an hour before, he was imagining the endless days of his life stretching out before him, without Nic.

And now she was offering him not just herself but a family of their own?

It was…

Well, it was everything.

"I have one condition." He shook his head. "No, that's not right. I have three."

"Tell me."

"No more separate decisions. It's killed me being apart these past months. Not seeing you. Not talking to you. Even if Olivia hadn't wanted to come here or the courts didn't agree, I'd have supported you. We'd have found a way."

"Okay," she said, her voice quiet. "What's the second condition?"

"You'd better not think we're stopping at one."

"One what?"

"Kid. I'm thinking we need at least three more. Maybe four."

"You gonna do something about that, Trace Withrow?"

He saw the deliciously wicked gleam in her vivid blue eyes and couldn't hold back any longer. Stepping forward, he laid his hands on her hips and pulled her against his body before he pressed his lips to hers. He gave her his answer as their lips met. "You better believe I am."

"And three?"

"Marry me, Nic. Make a life with me."

"That doesn't sound like a condition."

"What does it sound like?"

She smiled up at him, and he realized all the reasons he loved her were right there in her eyes. "An offer."

"Then I guess it is. Because I love you."

And right there, beside a cold mountain stream two thousand miles from where they first met, Trace heard the words he'd longed for his whole life.

"I love you, too, Trace. I will love you forever."

* * * * *

Look for more books in Addison Fox's miniseries, Wyoming Warriors, coming soon from Harlequin Romantic Suspense!